D0653338

POISED FOR THE KILL

The two wolves advanced side by side, the one-eyed gray to the left and the black monster to the right.

They paused a few feet from the gray dog, looking the field over with all the intelligence of military commanders. The black wolf sat down on his haunches, looking over every inch of the embattled gray dog, probing her strength and her weakness.

The wolf grinned fiendishly. They would kill the gray dog.

SNOW DOG

"The wild spirit of the country dominates the pages of this book. The characters are intensely lifelike; the suspense is keen."
—*Library Journal*

Snow Dog
by Jim Kjelgaard

A BANTAM SKYLARK BOOK®
TORONTO • NEW YORK • LONDON • SYDNEY • AUCKLAND

RL 8, 011-014

SNOW DOG

*A Bantam Skylark Book | published by arrangement with
Holiday House, Inc.*

PRINTING HISTORY

*Holiday House edition published 1948
15 printings through 1967*

Junior Literary Guild Edition 1948

Bantam Skylark edition | September 1980
2nd printing . . . . April 1981   3rd printing . . . . .May 1983

*Skylark Books is a registered trademark of Bantam Books, Inc.,
Registered in U.S. Patent and Trademark Office and elsewhere.*

*Bantam Books are published by Bantam Books, Inc. Its trade-
mark, consisting of the words "Bantam Books" and the por-
trayal of a rooster, is Registered in U.S. Patent and Trademark
Office and in other countries. Marca Registrada. Bantam
Books, Inc., 666 Fifth Avenue, New York, New York 10103.*

PRINTED IN THE UNITED STATES OF AMERICA

CW   12 11 10 9 8 7

Contents

Snow Dog

1. The Deserter

The north wind blew low across the snow fields, carrying powder snow before it and piling it on the drifts that lay like long, shadowed fingers in the lee of every tiny rise. With icy force the wind swept through the dark evergreens that marked the foot of a low, steep hill, and whistled up the slope, straight into the nose of the black wolf who sat there.

As large as a Great Dane, the wolf was in his battle-scarred prime. His ears were ripped and torn from a thousand fights. A ragged scar that ran from the base of his left ear to his left shoulder had grown in to pure white hair. The wolf elevated his grizzled muzzle to catch the full force of the wind, to read the story it carried to him.

The wild Carney River meadows started at the foot of the hill upon which he sat. Up those meadows was travelling a man with five pack dogs.

The black wolf's jowls curled in a snarl, and all his hate for men was contained in the sound that rippled from the depths of his chest. He had seen few men here, in this almost untravelled wilderness, but he knew about them. He had found out about their ways when he had been scarcely more than a cub, and had sat upon a sand bar watching a man approach. Suddenly there had been a blast of noise, a searing pain, and he had received the scar of shame which was still indelibly marked by the strip of white along his face and shoulder.

The black wolf had gone into one of his own hidden lairs to lick his wounds, and it was there that his hate of all men had been born. The next year had been one of very good hunting, and the young wolf's slatted ribs had filled out while his muscles became strong. That was the year the man who had shot him made the mistake of coming back, and of going moose hunting along one of the ridges which the black wolf had marked out for his own.

The wolf had struck his fresh trail, slinking behind spruces and windfalls where he knew he could not be seen. He himself had no need to see; his nose told him what was taking place. And, even while he stalked and hated, there was fear within him, fear of man, and of the weapons man carried. But he had been patient, and one day, when the man stumbled and fell face forward in the snow, the black wolf no longer feared. He had raced forward, a fleeting shadow black as death itself. Henceforth he knew that men, and especially fallen men, were not nearly as strong as the moose and caribou which the black wolf hunted regularly. They were not even as powerful as a small deer.

Even as he knew men, so did he know dogs. They were weak and powerless things, whose only strength lay in the fact that they travelled with men. On those four or five occasions when the black wolf had caught a dog away from a man, he had not needed half the speed in his legs to run it down nor half the strength in his jaws to kill it. Dogs were craven creatures who made a pretense of fighting but always screamed their fear of death when it was upon them.

The black wolf wriggled his nostrils. All five of the dogs out there on the meadows were large beasts, but four were no different from dogs which the wolf had met and killed. The fifth, a female, was the largest of all. The wolf licked his lips, and remembered the sheer pleasure he had felt when he killed dogs. Killing a dog was almost like striking down a man.

The black wolf stood up, drooping his tail in a half-circle and letting the wind plaster his thick fur closely against his powerful body. He turned and trotted down the opposite side of the hill, into a thick-set grove of small spruces. Fifteen gray wolves that had been lying idly in the thicket sprang to their feet, watching the black leader with cold but respectful eyes. The black wolf eyed the pack he led, then turned back to the wind that had brought him the story of man, pointed his muzzle at the clear blue sky, and howled.

It was a ghoulish sound, ringing and far-carrying, expressing all the hate in the black wolf's black brain. It told of his opinion of men, and of the dogs who were slaves of men. It rolled out on a savage note that emphasized the black wolf's intense longing to kill more men and more dogs. It carried to the man and dogs on the Carney meadows, and stopped them in their tracks.

Link Stevens, the man, turned toward the sound, balancing himself against a blast of wind. He was tall and straight, with black hair and brown eyes that had been set in so many solitary places where wind blew hard, and rain fell often, and snow lay deep, that already, at twenty, little wrinkles had formed around them. He looked at the pack dog nearest him, and back toward the sound again.

The dog whined uneasily, and tried to get nearer. Three of his pack mates crowded close to him. The fifth dog, a hundred-pound female whose outlines suggested a strong dash of both Husky and Irish wolfhound, lay down where she was. Link Stevens looked at her intently, and spoke over the heads of the other dogs.

"Don't be so high-hat, Queen. Come on up."

The big gray dog did not move, and Link's brown eyes softened a little. He had bought the big dog in Masland, the little frontier town in which he outfitted for his trap-lines on the Gander River, and he had known she was with pups when he had bought her. But he had got her at bargain rates, and he'd liked her looks. She was intelligent, strong, and courageous, but she was not a dog to make friends with anyone. Probably that was because she was due to whelp soon. Thoughtfully Link prodded the snow with the tip of one snowshoe. He'd win the big gray dog's friendship yet. He had gained and held the affection of every dog he'd had, and his dogs worked hard for him because they loved and respected him.

He looked back in the direction from which the wolf's howl had come, and a quizzical little smile twisted his lips. This was the Carney, home of the so-called devil wolf. Two years ago, so legend had it, a trapper named Chirikov had been killed by this devil wolf, a thing that could dodge bullets and assume any form at all. Well, devil wolf or not, it was still fifty miles to the Gander and almost four miles to Two-Bird Cabin, where he would stay that night.

"Let's get up the trail," he said amiably.

The four dogs rose to follow, but the big female

waited until they were twenty feet away before she moved. When she rose she did so cautiously, and the anxiety she felt showed in her eyes as she padded up the snowshoe trail the man was breaking. When she passed a secluded thicket, she looked wistfully at it. As she walked, she whimpered to herself so softly that even the keen-eared pack dogs did not hear her.

She had been born on a northern trail, and carried on the toboggan to which her mother was hitched until she, too, was big enough to run behind it. And she had learned bitterly the law of the trail: the strong go through but the weak must die. A natural mother, the big gray dog had never lost the memory of her first puppies. They, too, had been born on the trail, but they had been born in the custody of a swarthy little Frenchman whose only thought had been to move his loaded toboggan. Every additional pound had meant that it moved more slowly. With cold finality he had taken the squirming, helpless pups, knocked them on the head with the handle of his hunting knife, and left them dead in the snow. Now that horror was haunting her again.

She walked with deliberate slowness, letting the man and her pack mates keep ahead. She scarcely felt the thirty-five pound pack she carried. Again she looked longingly at a thicket, and took a little half-step toward it before unwillingly resuming her place in the line.

The big gray dog looked at Link Stevens. There was something about him she liked. But she had been with him only a week, and behind her were memories of too many harsh and cruel masters for her to give her complete confidence to anyone. She had to obey him; that was something born in her, something to which she gave no thought and over which she had no control. She had never known any life that did not have to do with the trail and the men who travelled it. She lowered her head and plodded on.

It was four o'clock in the afternoon, and the early northern twilight was already settling over the snow-covered wilderness when they came to Two-Bird Cabin. A ten by twelve log structure, with the front roof protruding to keep snow away from the door, the cabin nestled snugly among the spruces. In front was the river, the center of which was a swift-flowing channel that had not frozen. The pack dogs lay down, for they knew their day's work was done, and that presently they would be relieved of their packs. Maintaining her distance from the rest, the big female waited patiently.

Link Stevens walked down the half-circle of deep snow that had formed in front of the over-hanging roof, went into the cabin with his snow-shoes on, and came out with a water pail in his hand. He filled it at the river, carried it into the cabin, then came out and poked around in the deep snow until he worked down to the wood pile. A few minutes after he went into the cabin with an armload of wood, blue smoke began to curl out of the chimney. The all-important fire built, Link came out and began to remove the dog packs. No longer burdened, the first four shook themselves and began to sniff around the rabbit tracks near the cabin. Then Link knelt beside the big gray, sooth-ing her with stroking hands and pleasant voice.

"Poor old girl! Poor old Queenie! I know you're worried, but there's nothing to be afraid of. I'll take care of your babies when they come. I'll carry them myself."

The big dog looked gently at him, and licked his hands with her warm tongue. She liked this man, but remembered too many who saw dogs only as beasts of burden. If they could no longer bear those burdens they were summarily dispatched; only the very fit could go on the trail. Although she was grateful for this man's kindness, she neither understood nor trusted it.

Relieved of her pack, she trotted over near her team mates, but not too near. She did not trust them either. The big gray knew that the pack could combine, and use its united strength and cunning to pull down the game it sometimes ran. But there was no mercy or softness in them; they would pull down a weak pack mate, too.

Link Stevens came out of the cabin with five axe-hacked and still frozen pieces of moose meat in his hands. He knelt in the snow-free space under the protruding roof, and held up a piece of meat. Yuke, the big black leader of the five dogs, walked solemnly up, sat down in front of his master, and lifted a big paw to be shaken. He received his meat and backed into a corner of the cabin, where his flank was protected by a snow drift, to eat it.

"Tibby," Link called.

In their turns, Tibby, Lud, and Kena were fed, while the big gray dog sat patiently waiting her turn. This routine was as old as the trail itself, and she knew she could afford to be patient.

"Queen."

She advanced gravely, and sat down to hold up a feathery paw. The man reached out to tickle her ear.

"You're last, lady, but I saved the biggest piece for you, and it has a bone in it!"

She accepted the meat, and looked around at the other four dogs. Lying in the snow, always in some strategic place where at least one side was protected, they gnawed with relish at the hard, frozen meat. This routine was also as old as the trail. The dog who received his meat first would finish first. Then he would go all around to see what he could steal from the rest. The gray dog leaped over a small drift, plowed through a big one, and lay with her back against a spruce.

A little eddy of wind blew about her nostrils, and anxiously, as though the breeze might contain some hidden message, she raised her head to sniffle into it. Then she fell on the moose meat with rending jaws, tearing it off in chunks and swallowing the chunks whole.

Yuke finished, and stalked stiff-leggedly over to where Tibby was still busily tearing his meat to pieces. A growl warned him away. As though he didn't care anyway, Yuke walked indifferently past. In turn he visited Lud and Kena, but was similarly warned off. Following the trail the big gray had made, he came over to look down on her.

She stopped eating, and lay with her motionless head raised over the half-finished meal. Well-recognized trail etiquette governed this procedure. She should growl, and warn the interloper that she would fight if he insisted on trespassing. Then he would either accept her challenge or go away.

But she did not feel like growling. With a sudden, mad rush she was out of the snow and upon her team mate. Surprised, Yuke braced himself to meet the charge. They came together, and reared with flailing paws and probing jaws that sought each other's throats. There was about the big female a strange madness, an all-consuming rage. She wanted nothing near her.

"Yuke! Queen!"

Link Stevens' commanding voice came dimly to

the gray dog. She did not see him standing in the cabin's doorway, nor did she see him bend to pick up a club. With desperate fury she bored in, wishing only to kill. There was no thought save that she must kill, and she scarcely felt the sharp blow as Link tapped her smartly across the nose, nor scarcely heard Yuke's pained yelp as the club descended, much harder, on him. He tried to back away, but the big female crowded him hard. No longer was she a creature conditioned by thousands of years of living with men. She was a beast, fighting viciously for the preservation of the lives within her. She started to leap at something in front of her. Then, suddenly, the mists in her brain cleared. She saw her master, and heard his soothing voice.

"It's all right, Queen. He's gone and won't be back. Take it easy. You'll be all right."

Link Stevens knew the harshness of the snow trails, but he had not let that harshness rob him of his own finer sensibilities. Nor had it dulled his admiration for the dogs who did the work on those snow trails. He spoke again.

"Go back to your supper, Queen, and don't worry. I'll take care of you." With a reassuring pat he turned and went into the cabin.

The big gray dog wagged her furred tail gently as she watched him go, then trotted back to her unfinished meal. But while she had fought, Kena had stolen it. Trying to look innocent, but obviously guilty, he lay in the snow, gnawing the last shreds of meat from the treasured bone. For one fleeting moment the big gray dog again felt a consuming rage, but it passed. She had more important things on her mind.

The flickering candle which had lighted the cabin's frosted window was suddenly extinguished as Link Stevens sought his bunk. A round moon rose palely to light the wilderness, and throw every spruce tree into an unreal pattern of sharp angles and soft shadows. Queen still sat aloof, but the four other dogs were restless and eager. Yuke whined expectantly, and ran a little circle around his team mates. Then, as though they knew exactly where they were going, they left the cabin and started into the forest.

Slowly the big gray followed them, for she knew what this meant. Day was a time for work, but night was a time for pleasure, and now the dogs would take theirs. A snowshoe rabbit darted like a pale ghost across a moon-sprayed clearing, and the pack was after it in yelling pursuit. Now the dogs were no longer chattels of man, but hunters much as their ancestors had been ten thousand years before them.

The rabbit dashed through a thick clump of alders. The others raced around it in pursuit, but Queen stopped, uneasy and restless. She thought of Link Stevens, and trotted back to the cabin.

From the forest, the yelling of the rabbit-chasing pack came dimly to her. It was an old hunting paean, one that swelled when the dogs raced across an opening, and faded when they were in the thick brush. Queen looked toward the sound, and back at the cabin. She whined pleadingly. When nothing stirred within the cabin, she trotted over to the trail they had broken that day. Memories of the enticing thickets she had seen returned with overwhelming force.

She raised one front paw, then the other, while an agony of indecision wrenched her. Work dogs had few laws, but the foremost of these demanded service to the death for one's master. Old instincts and new yearnings battled with that certain knowledge.

When Queen made her decision, it was an irrevocable one. She turned and trotted back down the trail over which she had labored with a pack on her back. And, now that she had definitely decided to break all ties with men, a great cunning came out of that half of her that had never been tamed. It was her wild, free nature, and she now coupled it with what she knew of men.

She was perfectly aware of the fact that, on snow, she would leave a trail that could be followed. She also knew best how to hide that trail. The big dog ran down the packed snowshoe path, a fleeting shadow in the night. She paused when she came to a thicket, but looked questioningly back over her shoulder and ran on. Men had travelled this trail once and would again. She did not want to be near them.

Queen raced on until she came to a place where a herd of caribou had crossed the trail and climbed a ridge. Without hesitation she turned aside on the caribou tracks, and followed them. Two miles farther on, at the very summit of a small hill, she caught up with the herd. Scenting her, the caribou plunged away in the darkness.

Now she was in unbroken snow. It was hard going, but she was used to travel, and knew a dozen small tricks that were useful.

Dawn broke over the wilderness. Moose snorted and moved out of her way. A red squirrel chattered at her from a tree, and a jay scolded her as it flew away. Wet and tired, but at last feeling secure, the gray dog stopped on top of a rock cliff from which the wind had blown all the snow. She looked down into a thicket of spruce, and her eye was attracted by a windfall where a number of large fallen spruces lay in a tangled heap. Small trees and brush had found a rooting place among them. It looked dry, warm, and comfortable. Gratefully the tired dog crawled under the bole of a huge log, and into the windfall's dim depths. Leaves and forest trash had blown in there, but little snow had fallen. She lay down and began to lick her wet fur.

Link Stevens woke up in the early pre-dawn blackness of a winter's morning. For a few moments he lay awake on the bunk, and drew the blankets closer about him to shut out the intense cold. He yawned, and turned over drowsily. It was still fifty miles to his trap-lines on the Gander, and in this deep snow they'd be fifty trying miles. Still, there had been no heavy blizzards on this trip, and he was grateful for that. He thought of the pack horses he'd left on the Gander meadows. Even though they hadn't been able to travel in this snow, they'd be all right. They knew where the best grass was, and could easily paw down to it. Probably would even have grown fat. . . .

Finally he swung his feet to the floor, ran across it, stuffed tinder into the stove, lighted it, laid a couple of wood chunks on top, and hurried back to the warmth of his bed. As soon as the cabin had warmed, he got up to prepare his breakfast of moose steak and hot cakes. The slow dawn was just breaking when he went to the door with a dog pack in each hand.

"Hi—ya!" he called.

Yuke, Tibby, Lud, and Kena came out of the sleeping holes they had dug in the snow, yawning and stretching, and shook themselves. With wagging tails they trotted up to the cabin, waiting for their packs to be put on.

"Queen!" Link called.

Yuke looked questioningly over his shoulder, obviously displeased because the fifth member of his pack was missing. Link called again, louder.

"Queen! Where are you?"

He felt a cold sinking in the pit of his stomach and turned to drop the dog packs back in the cabin. On this mid-winter trip to Masland and back, he had left the Gander with only four dogs, none of which was exceptional. He had bought the big female partly because he needed another pack animal which would also be of some use on the toboggan, but largely because he had liked her looks. He'd hoped her pups would grow as big and strong, and be as intelligent, as the mother. Now, having ignored all his advances, she'd gone into the wilderness alone. He couldn't leave her there; he couldn't leave any dog with helpless puppies. Questioningly he looked down at the four remaining dogs.

They were work animals, not hunters, and about the only animals that ever interested them were snowshoe rabbits. He could take them along while he hunted for Queen, but they'd be more of a nuisance than a help. He tied all four dogs to separate trees, so they wouldn't get in a fight, and went back into the cabin.

He made himself two steak sandwiches, wrapped them in a piece of cloth, stepped out from beneath the overhanging roof, and put on his snowshoes. He mounted the drift in front of the cabin, and stood a moment while he tried to decide which way to go. Last night he had heard the pack coursing rabbits. Probably Queen had been

with them, at least for a while. It did not seem
likely, since she had more important matters to
think of, that she would waste much time on rabbit
trails. Still, he had better go see.

Link snowshoed into the spruces, casting back
and forth until he picked up the trail left by the
pack. He knelt to study it, and thought he could
detect the paw prints of only four dogs in the
ruffled snow. He might be mistaken. It was possible that Queen had run all the way with the pack,
and gone on from wherever they had either caught
or lost the rabbit. Link followed the tracks, going
around thickets that the rabbit and dogs had
dodged through. He found a spot of blood and
some bits of white fur where the pack had finally
overtaken its quarry. From there the trail led directly back to the cabin. No dog had run on into the
forest.

Link furrowed his brow, and tried to eliminate
all the places where the missing dog could not be.
Certainly she would seek a thicket, or, because it
would be ideal for her purposes, she might look for
a windfall. However, when there were countless
windfalls all about. . . .

Link made a wide circle completely around the
cabin. No dog tracks except those he had already
crossed broke the snow. He stopped, baffled.
Then a smile flickered across his face and a warm
chuckle broke from him. That Queen! She was the
smartest dog!

Of course she had deliberately hidden her own
tracks; the one way she could do that was by running down the trail they had broken yesterday.
Link chuckled again, and all the warm feeling he
had for dogs—especially dogs in trouble—seemed
to make this task a particularly welcome one.
When he found Queen, he would treat her very

kindly, take care of her puppies, and so be sure to win her affection.

He snowshoed down the trail, travelling slowly and with his eyes down. He was sure Queen would have left the trail; she wanted to get far away from any place where men travelled. Furthermore, when she left the trail, she would have done her best to leave it in such a way that her own tracks would remain undetected. Link chuckled again, then stopped to call.

"Queen!"

For a few seconds he waited, and when nothing appeared, he called again. Still no dog came, and Link went on down the trail. He kept his eyes down, trying to miss nothing on either side. A deer and several moose had crossed the trail since he had come up yesterday, and a herd of splay-footed caribou had ambled across to climb a hill. Link grimaced. He didn't like caribou; they rambled all over, and once they'd been on even a packed snowshoe trail they left it in such a mess that invariably a new trail had to be broken out. He walked over the caribou tracks, balancing himself precariously on the rough snow, and missing entirely the dog tracks in their midst.

He went on to the farthest point at which he thought Queen might have turned from the trail, and then, just to make certain, travelled two miles beyond that point. At last he stopped, resting on his snowshoes while he tried to fathom the mystery.

He was positive that she had left the trail, and, because he had tried to look at everything, he was also sure that she had hidden her tracks so well that he'd overrun them. Nothing remained but a general search, and even before he started Link knew that finding a lost dog in this wilderness would be considerably more difficult than locating a missing needle in a haystack. But as long as there was even a slight chance of finding her, he would continue to look. He was sure she would respond if she heard him call. He had shouted frequently and loudly; therefore Queen must be so far off the trail that she had not heard him at all.

Without doubt she had crawled into the most secluded spot she could find. But had she gone east of the trail, or west? There was no positive way of knowing. He picked up a bit of snow and tossed it into the air. When it landed on his own west side, he crossed the river flat and went up a wooded hill. Moose, deer, caribou, and numberless rabbits had so marked the snow that finding any one track was almost hopeless. He came to a dense windfall, and called again. No answer.

He continued on, a mile from the trail, then cut back toward the cabin. Patiently he investigated every windfall, either climbing them or going completely around them to make sure the missing dog was not beneath. He grinned faintly. When that Queen dog set out to hide herself, she did a good job!

A covey of clouds scudded across the sky and Link looked up anxiously. More snow would make his task completely hopeless. He hurried on, but when he returned to the cabin that night, he had found no trace of the lost dog. He went out the next day, and the next. When he returned to the cabin on the third night, great feathery flakes of snow were already drifting out of an overcast sky.

That night a north wind began to blow up, howling around the cabin, driving the falling snow before it and adding it to the drifts. For a long time Link lay awake in his bunk, and when he finally went to sleep, troubled dreams of the lost dog chased each other through his slumber. The next morning, when he went to the door, he knew he would never find her.

The snow lay piled in new drifts, whorls, and windrows. It had been driven hard by the wind, until even the snowshoe trail leading away from the cabin was only a faintly marked trace. Glumly Link strapped their packs on the dogs, dividing Queen's load among the four and himself. Before he started his lonely journey to the Gander, he left a big chunk of moose meat in front of the door.

The gray dog *might* come back.

2. Under the Windfall

The big gray dog under the windfall lay very still.
Here the storm did not strike. Outside, the wailing
north wind still lashed the forest, carrying frost
particles with it and leaving a rime of frost on the
north side of every hardwood tree with which it
came in contact. Bitter cold, borne on the wings of
that wind, penetrated to the inner sap bark of the
trees; they creaked and groaned as the torturing
frost crept in and congealed their very life's blood.

But cold and wind had been understood so long
by the gray dog that they could bring no terror, nor
even much concern. Many cold nights on the trail
she had slept in the same hole with another dog,
and she knew the added warmth that could be
generated by two living beings that stayed together. In addition, her maternal sense told her of
the abject helplessness of the squirming mites beside her, and she knew that their only hope of
survival lay in the protection she could offer. All
that day and all night the mother dog lay quietly,
shielding her young, and it was well into the morning of the next day before she arose.

She stood up for just a few seconds, and then
only because she had a consuming desire to see

the tiny things which she held so dear, and for which she had endured so much. Her tail wagged gently as she looked down at the pups.

All three were tiny, with budding pink ears that seemed to be sprouting from the soft skulls in which they were imbedded. Black muzzles terminated in little black noses, and unseeing blue eyes strove earnestly to penetrate a world which consisted of the rock at their backs, the log over them, and three feet of dark passageway that led to the first curve that must be taken to get out of the windfall. Even that was an immense and unknown world for things so small and helpless.

Two of the pups were whitish-gray, with stubby, black-tipped tails that curled like caterpillars from their tiny sterns. Yet, fragile though they were, there was a perfection and a symmetry to their smallness that seemed to bear out the anticipation and pride in the big gray dog's eyes. If their legs and paws were clumsy, they were also in almost perfect proportion to the chests and backs supporting those legs. Their spines were long and straight, their chests well formed. Even in infancy the two pups' characteristics, like signs along a highway, presaged the things that would be after they had had time to travel a little way.

Within the third puppy the Husky strain was dominant. He was the color of steel, except for curving, parallel streaks of white and black that ran from each of his eyes almost to the end of his muzzle, and gave the effect of a mask across his face. Even now his ears were more pointed than those of his brothers. If their chests were wide and deep, his was just a little wider and deeper. His front legs, although puppy-soft, were straight and strong, and his rear legs, even now, foretold unusual staying power. His muzzle came to a blunter point than did the muzzles of the other two, and there seemed to be more strength in his jaw and head.

Queen raised her head toward the top of the windfall, as though giving thanks for sons so fine and strong. Then she lay down again, using her warm body to shelter them from the cold. When the gray pup with the masked face tried to crawl from the nest, she nudged him gently back. The mother dog dozed.

Ten minutes later she was wide awake, startled and nervous, conscious of the fact that something was wrong. She swung her head to the puppies beside her, and saw only the two silver-gray ones sleeping on top of each other. The third, he of the black and white face, had already gone adventuring. Pulling himself with his front legs and pushing with his back, almost helpless, unable to see, he had squirmed eighteen inches into the depths of the windfall. Now, trying to use eyes that could see nothing, ears that were attuned to almost nothing, and paws which had felt nothing except the warmth of his mother, he was trying to climb over a small stick that lay near. Gently the big gray dog seized him by the scruff of his neck and dragged him back. She lay quietly in the dark depths of her refuge, worrying as any mother does about a child who, at too early an age, shows signs of waywardness.

Suddenly Queen rose from the nest, bristling, and moved away from the puppies so their scent would not interfere with another that had come to her nostrils. The wind that crept under the windfall and around the various curves within had brought her an alien scent, one she feared.

The mother dog raced silently out of the twisting tunnel she had followed into this snug haven.

She stood at the entrance, eyes blazing and ruff erect, ready to fight. Only she could protect the pups. To do so she would, if necessary, give her own life.

Two minutes later, the wolverene she had scented came in sight. It faced her, a squat, powerful beast that gave out a sickening odor, and looked at her with weak, blinking eyes while it tried in its own mind to decide whether there was anything to be gained in trying to force its way into this dark place wherein there was something to eat. With all the fierce courage of a bear, and all the bloody savagery of the weasel whose pattern it followed, the wolverene would usually fight if so doing would bring some gain.

The big gray dog took a step forward, keeping her head down to protect her throat in the struggle that might start any second. A curdling growl rolled from her throat, and her heavy lips curled back to expose slashing fangs. But about her was something even more dangerous: an aura which any enemy powerful enough to challenge her could understand. When the mother dog started to defend her pups, only death could end the battle.

The wolverene chattered its teeth, then beat a hasty retreat. Throughout the ages wolverenes had learned that they were nearly invincible, and most of the time they upheld that reputation with their actions. But not when they faced an enraged mother as big as the gray dog. There was no reason for a fight to the death when that death might be your own. Like all tyrants, the wolverene preferred to find small, weak things upon which to exercise its strength and ferocity.

The big gray dog remained at the windfall's mouth a few minutes longer, until she was sure that her enemy had gone. Then, and only then, did she return to the pups. She found that during her absence he of the masked face had managed to squirm three feet from the nest. Heedless of the outraged squeals that ensued when her sharp teeth pricked the soft skin on his neck, Queen picked the wanderer up and firmly carried him back to his place. When she lay down to warm the shivering pups, she did so worriedly. It was enough to assume all the care of three helpless babies. But to have one of them such a problem . . . .

All that night the big dog crouched over her puppies, unmindful of the hunger pangs in her own belly and of the fact that she had eaten nothing since Link Stevens had given her some frozen moose meat forty-eight hours ago. She was consumed by a desperate worry.

It was not for herself, or for the hunger that cut her like a burning knife. The mother dog understood such pangs. Often, when there had been no food on the toboggan, she had gone hungry for two or three days. This was different, and more important, and most urgent. Her pups, clinging desperately to a new and wholly uncertain life, had to eat. They had only one source of food, and if she did not eat she could not feed them.

In the morning Queen rose, bending her muzzle into the frozen air that crept under the windfall, then looking back at her pups. In a sudden fit of temper she returned to pick up the masked-face puppy and put him back with his brothers. The big gray dog growled fiercely. Then, as though resigned to the knowledge that the pup would pay no attention anyhow, she trotted to the opening by which she had entered the windfall and faced the winter wilderness. She looked at the snow-laden trees, sure of what she had to do but not knowing how to go about doing it.

She had hunted before, but always in the company of pack mates. Those hunts had been glorious, mad chases over the snow, and at their end she had helped pull down the luckless deer or caribou, or ripped to shreds the rabbit that happened to be in front of the coursing pack. Now she was alone, faced with the positive necessity of getting food with none to help her. The big gray dog ventured into the winter woods.

She travelled cautiously but swiftly, watching, listening, and scenting, as she strove to locate game. A snowshoe rabbit leaped up before her, and she gave instant, violent chase, trying in one great burst of speed to run down and kill this thing which, at the moment, spelled salvation for her pups. The rabbit flashed through a grove of ground-hugging spruces, and the big gray dog drew up in bewildered dismay. With an entire pack running, it had always been easy to catch a rabbit. Now, unexplainably, it was impossible. Among the pack, there had been one or more dogs gifted with a talent for following ground scent. Queen had never run her game except by sight, and when it was no longer in sight she could not find it.

She wandered disconsolately on, the desperate fear within her increasing as she went farther without catching anything. When she stalked a cheeky and chattering red squirrel, it let her approach to within six feet and then jumped to safety in a tree. Trying to catch a spruce hen, she crept to within a yard and a half, only to see it fly away. Twice more she coursed rabbits, without success. Then she caught another scent.

Mingled with the smell of the caribou was the odor of something else, something that made the gray dog's ruff bristle even while she advanced. It was the old scent of the black wolf and his pack, the beasts who had killed the caribou, eaten as much as they wanted, then spurned the rest as carrion while they went in search of live, hot game. The gray dog feared the wolf scent, but even more she feared the specter of her puppies going hungry. She crept cautiously nearer.

A white weasel snarled at her from inside the torn carcass of the bull, then fled in undulating leaps over the snow when the big gray dog did not hesitate. She reared, placing her front paws on the dead bull and trying with her ears, nose, and eyes to locate anything she might possibly have to battle before partaking of this bounty. There was nothing, and she fell to ripping off shreds of frozen meat and swallowing them whole. Having eaten all she could, she trotted back to the den under the windfall.

She approached anxiously, worriedly, ready to fight anything at the windfall should fighting be necessary. It was not. There was no odor around the entrance save that of herself, the three puppies, and the wolverene. The gray dog ran under the windfall.

The silver-gray puppies lay in the nest, huddled against one another for warmth. The steel-gray one had again pushed himself out, and on paws so weak they would not bear even the weight of his tiny body he had started on another exploring trip. Firmly the big gray dog picked him up by the nape of the neck, carried him back to his brothers, deposited him beside them, and lay down to feed her brood.

It was mid-morning of the next day before she

left the windfall again, and trotted straight to the remains of the caribou. Then, after two weeks, the rest of the caribou was gone. However, the end of that week brought the chinook.

The north wind, that had wailed and moaned almost without cessation for two weeks, died suddenly. In its place came the west wind, no slashing, biting blast but a questing breeze that carried with it a promise of warmth to be. At high noon the wilderness still shivered and recoiled from the fierce breath it had known so steadily and so long, but by evening the snow had softened. Little driblets of water ran from the melting snow on top of the windfall to fall in the forest trash beneath, and as each drop of water fell it splattered in a soft, reassuring way. The big gray dog sat up to watch, and the next morning she left very early on her usual hunt.

In the nest under the windfall the three puppies saw her go, then the two silver-gray ones lay down to sleep. The burned-steel pup with the masked face lay down beside them, but he kept peering over the backs of the two in the direction his mother had taken. He would bend his tiny nose to the back of a brother, then look toward the path his mother had taken.

In the ten days since they had been born under the windfall the pups had grown steadily, and now even a casual eye could see a definite indication of the sturdy creatures they would be. Offspring of their big mother and a fierce, wayward staghound father who had left a trail of broken canine hearts along ten thousand miles of snow trail, they had inherited the size and weight of both. The Husky in his ancestry had bequeathed his own shape to the masked-face puppy, and already lithe grace was evident. Also noticeable were other things.

There was not too much difference in their sizes, but the Husky puppy was definitely the largest. Also, although all were now able to see, the steel-gray pup had been able to distinguish the log over them, the trash upon which they lay, and the outlines of his mother and brothers, a full day before the other two had seen anything.

He rose again, looking over his brothers at the windfall's exit. Almost from the hour he was born there had been a deep sense within him that had nothing to do with sight, or hearing, or scent, or touch. That sense had told him of enticing things outside the windfall, and those things were irresistible lures to which he had to respond. The puppy whined, rising on his still-clumsy legs and trying to make himself tall so he could see better. He looked down at his brothers, and they stirred gently when he licked them with his warm tongue. The steel-gray puppy tumbled out of the nest. His worm-like tail wagged back and forth as he started awkwardly toward the windfall's exit.

A drop of water spilled from a log squarely onto his back. The puppy sat down, squatting in the path his mother had worn and trying to decide what unknown thing had come upon him from nowhere. He tried to turn so he could see his back, and fell on his fat side. The puppy lay there, dozing. Ten minutes later he was up again, striving toward the outside world that was so irresistible. An instinct old as the race of dogs kept him in the path his mother had worn. Here one member of the pack had gone. Here another could go.

A foot-wide patch of snow that had drifted down through the windfall blocked his path. Again the puppy sat down, regarding this marvel with his newly opened eyes and striving with his puppy brain to find a proper place for anything so strange.

He put his head out to touch it, lost his balance and tumbled into it. The puppy wriggled and squirmed across the snow, and when he reached the other side he sat down proudly, as though he personally were responsible for something grand and wonderful. Then he lay down for another nap.

Again he rose, struggling toward the exit and the things his inner sense told him he would find there. A mouse whose hidden home lay in the dark depths of the windfall squeaked and rustled, and the puppy turned in amazement to regard the sound. He wriggled his tiny nose, instinctively trying to catch the odor of the mouse, and was puzzled because he could not. His nose was not yet developed to the point where he could detect any scent save those which were near and very powerful. The puppy lay down beside a stick that lay crosswise of the trail his mother used, and crawled the length of it while he probed its possibilities with his paws and nose. Finally, making a supreme effort, he crawled over it. Two feet farther on he reached the entrance to the windfall and the gray dog's den.

The puppy composed himself, one front paw over the other and his jaws parted slightly as he regarded the scene before him. A steep valley down which a brook coursed dropped sharply away in a series of frozen waterfalls and rapids. Large spruces with spear-like tops and feathered branches crowded the valley and marched in ragged order over the tops of the ridges on either side. An unbroken pattern of robin's egg blue, the sky seemed to curve in a protecting shield over the wilderness panorama, and to let the sun slide down its sides in order that warmth might be brought to a land that was too long frozen.

The puppy sat happily, enjoying the things his

inner sense had told him existed out here. Only they were far more wonderful than he had ever believed. So engrossed was he in the scene that he did not see the slight shadow that floated beside him.

It was cast by a day-hunting great horned owl. The owl had been out all night, and had struck half a dozen times at the snowshoe rabbits which were more numerous than any other animal here in this frozen land where only the powerful, the fleet, or the marvellously fecund had a chance of surviving. Each time the rabbits had eluded him. Then the owl had swooped at a spruce hen that was roosting in an evergreen, but a second before he struck, a pine marten that had also been stalking the hen seized it, and dropped to the soft snow beneath the tree. Enraged, trying to strike the marten, the owl had found only the black hole into which it had gone with its pirated meal.

Cruising over the valley in front of the windfall, the owl saw the wind-ruffled fur of the steel-gray puppy. It turned on silent wings and banked for its strike. The owl's murderous eyes were fixed with concentrated intensity on the puppy. Without even a whisper of noise it descended, and only when it was almost on him did the puppy look up. With no conscious thought, but instinct that acted even swifter, he recognized his danger, and awkwardly turned to run. He felt a raking stab in his shoulder, then went tumbling end over end to bring up against a log with such force that the breath in his body was squeezed out in one single gasp. His mother had arrived.

Coming back to the windfall after a partially successful hunt in which she had managed to catch a muskrat, she had seen the owl while she was still some yards away. The big gray dog leaped

forward, and when she was still ten feet away
launched her mighty body from the spring-steel
muscles given her by endless days and endless
miles on the trail. Closing her jaws about the owl,
she struck the claw-scratched puppy with her
shoulder and sent him sprawling.

The puppy rose painfully, and turned to see the
owl flailing his mother with huge wings. The gray
dog closed her jaws more tightly and hung on,
grinding her teeth deeper into the warm flesh. The
owl extended a claw, sought and found a hold on
her left ear. When he exerted pressure, the talons
on the end of his clamp-like claw met through the
mother dog's ear. The owl's beak opened and
closed with a continuous snapping, like the repeated clicking of a toy gun, as it sought a vital spot
on its enemy. The big dog loosened her jaws,
lunged, and closed her mouth farther up on the
feathered body. She squeezed. The owl's beating
wings stopped, as though they had been fanned by
a wind that suddenly died.

Queen dropped the dead owl and leaped to her
puppy. She nuzzled him, and licked away the few
drops of blood that oozed from the raking scratch
inflicted by the owl's talon. Then, grasping him
gently by the loose fur on his neck, she ducked
under the log that led to the windfall nest. As an
afterthought, she laid the puppy down and went
back to carry the owl beneath the windfall. It was
not food she liked, but it was food, and that was
all-important now. She tenderly gathered her
puppy up again.

He dangled from his mother's jaws, riding contentedly as the ache left his lungs and normal
breath crept back into them. The gray dog placed
him beside his brothers, lay down herself, and the
puppies fed. Their bellies full, the two silver-gray

pups lay down to sleep, but for a long time the mask-face sat wakeful beside them. Through him trembled a great excitement inspired both by his visit to the edge of the windfall and his mother's fight with the horned owl.

He would have liked to be in that fight. Sitting up, bracing his fat self with his fore paws, he peered toward the entrance, and whined uneasily. His first adventure into the world he had yearned to see had been a very satisfying one, but if it had left him with an inspired sense of fulfillment it had also imprinted caution upon his brain. Wonderful as the wilderness was, it had its dangers.

Every day, for two months, Queen went out to hunt. Always before she had hunted for pleasure; her food had been furnished. Now she had to hunt for food, not only for herself but for the three puppies whose lives were so infinitely precious. They were her world, and all her world. As she hunted, the big gray dog learned how to do so cunningly and successfully.

Instead of bounding after snowshoe rabbits, and sometimes catching them but more often missing, it was far easier to crouch beside a travelled run and leap when a rabbit hopped past. She learned the places where spruce hens fed on the ground, and how to ambush them in such places. There was always a chance of catching a squirrel that had ventured too far from a tree, or a muskrat that had travelled too far from its water refuge. Several times the big dog chased deer and caribou, but failed to catch and pull one down. She was a consistently successful hunter only with small game.

In spite of her prowess, Queen steadily became more thin and gaunt. In their sheltered nest under the windfall the pups grew like corn in a rich and watered garden. They were piling out of the nest now, playing their puppyish games, exploring their own tiny world, and always waiting for her to return from a hunt. When she did, all three were there to leap upon her as they ceaselessly demanded food and still more food.

Instead of hunting only once a day now, Queen had to go out morning and night. She remembered the wolverene, and on her various expeditions she crossed the scents of other fearsome creatures which came near—far too near—the windfall. At no time did she dare stay away for more than an hour or two. As a consequence the game near the windfall was growing scarce. She had to hunt desperately to get enough.

The puppies under the windfall continued to play, and to run a few feet after their mother when she went through the tunnel on her hunting trips. The mother dog had schooled two of her babies well; they remained and would remain where they were safe. The mask-face was more of a problem. He had learned by bitter experience that the world can be a rough place, but even harsh lessons leave no lasting impression on the very young.

For a week now no melting snow had dribbled through the windfall and dampened its floor. A white trillium that had somehow found a rooting place on one of the mossy logs burst into full bloom, and strained toward the sun that filtered through a crack between two logs. Spring had come.

One morning the three puppies watched their mother start out to hunt and, as always, followed her a few feet down the tunnel. Only this time they did not turn back. They would have done so, but when the silver-gray pups sat down to watch their mother disappear they looked at their dark brother instead of back at the nest. He sat with his feet braced, his pointed ears as erect as he could hold them, as he stared toward the windfall's entrance. Then he took a few more hesitant steps forward.

All the old yearning to go out and see what was there had returned to him with overwhelming force. Only dimly remembered was the striking owl; deep within his brain was a tiny cell that would be perpetually devoted to watching for danger from the sky.

When he advanced, his two brothers cautiously followed. The steel-gray puppy walked more surely this time, and more steadily. The growth he had already achieved bore out fully the promise he had held as a squirming pup. He was still clumsy, but he was also big-boned and heavy. His muzzle was more pointed. His ears had a tendency to droop, but later they would stand sharply erect. He stood a full inch taller, and was two pounds heavier, than either of his brothers.

Also, now within him were powers that had not been his when he had made his first uncertain journey to the mouth of the windfall. Before he heard them rustle or squeak, his nose told him that the mouse family still lived under the log beside the passageway. He was aware of the weasel that had come to hunt those mice, and of the lynx which had started to climb through the windfall until it had caught the scent of the gray dog and fled hastily in the other direction.

The steel-gray puppy came to the entrance. He lay down there, far enough under the log so nothing could strike him from the sky, but far enough out so he could see. Now he looked at a green world. No longer shackled by its ice fetters, the little stream played and danced, and hurled itself over the series of falls with a reckless joy that was like a new-found happiness in living. Green grass

grew wherever there were no trees, and a red
cardinal flitted about high in a spruce. The puppy
turned to look at his two brothers. Amazed by their
own daring, they were right behind him under the
windfall, bending and craning their necks the better to see out.

Suddenly the masked-face puppy became
aware of a new scent and a new animal approach-
ing. It was a heavy, oily scent, and it marched
ahead of the beast from which it sprang like a
herald announcing the approach of royalty. The
puppy shuffled his front paws uneasily. His first
excursion into the unknown had taught him that it
was well to be cautious. Still, there was nothing of
danger, or threat, in the scent of this beast. A few
minutes later it came in sight.

It was a massive, heavy-set thing, with a huge
head surmounted by small ears and marked with
tiny eyes. Its gait was a shuffling walk. Its fur was
long and brown, intermixed with silver-gray hairs.
The beast grunted like a pig, and restlessly
brushed its nose against the earth as if seeking
something it might have lost. It hooked its mighty
fore paws into a log, and sent great splinters flying.
Then it zestfully licked up the small white grubs
that crawled beneath the rotten wood. The thing
came on, still grunting and dipping its nose to the
ground.

Opposite the windfall, it stopped to stare with
weak, questioning eyes at the puppy watching it
so quietly. Within the opening, the two light-
colored puppies turned and slunk back to their
nest. The steel-gray puppy remained, still scenting no threat in this mighty creature, and over-
whelmingly curious to know more about it. It
came near, and bent a shaggy head three times as
large as the puppy to sniffle at him. The puppy

rose, wagged a friendly tail, and lapped his warm, wet tongue over the monster's nose. The thing wrinkled its nostrils, then, as though the pup was unworthy of any more attention, wheeled and went on its grunting, head-swinging way.

The puppy watched it go, and within his brain filed the scent of this particular creature as something which he need not fear. He felt instinctively that it meant no harm to him. What he did not know was that he had made the acquaintance of the mightiest monarch of them all—King Grizzly.

3. The Hunters

Long before the spring sun grew warm, and
melted the deep snows into water that crept over
and into the earth, ran down every little ditch and
crevice, filled every hole with water, and swelled
the streams and rivers, the black wolf saw his pack
begin to break up. Two by two they went, always a
male and a female together, as they responded to
the spring's imperious decree that new life must
come to replace that which had died in the cold
and the snow.

The wolves did not abandon the pack in a group,
nor even at the same time. Coursing through that
vast stretch of wilderness which they held by reason of strength, a wolf might drop behind the pack
and sit upon some little knoll or hillock. Its mate
would range on for a way, but before it had gone far
it would leave the pack and return to the one who
waited. The older wolves usually left the rest near
the same dens they had used last year, but the four
young wolves in the pack ranged out to find new
homes as far from their parents as they could get.
By the time the chinook struck, the black wolf's
pack was scattered over a hundred square miles of
wilderness, as it should have been. Each pair of

wolves with young to rear would need a wide area in which to run down and kill game for cubs whose appetites would have no end. Two pairs of wolves in the same territory would overrun each other's hunting grounds and eventually the stronger pair would win all.

The snow was melting fast but still lay heavy on the ground when the black wolf and another male, a big gray brute with a scarred chest and one eye, found themselves alone. Both wolves, the previous year, had had mates and young, but lost them to forces which even their age and experience could not control. A wandering trapper, packing out from his northern trap-lines, had found the one-eyed wolf's den, shot the female, and captured the pups. The gray wolf had only been able to watch helplessly from a hidden thicket, and to grieve at the den afterward.

The black wolf's four pups had been well grown when disaster overtook them. Along with his mate, he had taken the pups on a hunt. They had sighted a caribou calf whose mother had already fallen to the black wolf, and coursed the terrified creature through a mile or so of forest. Finally the panting, big-eyed calf sought refuge on an overhanging bank of a swollen, rushing river, and there he had turned to defend himself as best he could.

The black wolf had stayed back. Knowing that the cubs would have to meet and pull down much larger and fiercer beasts, he realized that killing the calf would be the finest possible training for his young. With gurgling puppy snarls that sometimes ended in squeaks, the four cubs closed in. More solicitous of their welfare than the black wolf, the gray mother went in with them. The agile calf struck with his hooves and butted with his baby head, and might have escaped from the cubs had not the mother darted ahead to show them the correct killing technique. Just as she leaped at the calf's throat, a long section the overhanging bank, undermined by spring erosion, caved in and carried both the attacking wolves and the defending calf into the raging water. The black wolf had been able only to go to the edge and peer into the swirling river. He had never seen his mate or cubs again.

Both of the old male wolves might have taken new mates if they had wanted them. Strong and savage, they could easily have defeated any of the young males who fought among themselves for last year's females. But neither of them particularly wanted a young she, or any mate not as experienced and savage as himself. In addition, both were past that period when a mate is all-important.

They ranged together through the wilderness, going where they pleased except near any wolf den. That was taboo. Lynxes, marten, fisher, weasels, wolverenes, and mink would kill wolf cubs if they could do so safely. The she wolves had enough trouble guarding and feeding their young, and any alien wolf who even annoyed her immediately put himself beyond the pale of the pack law, and became an outcast to be hunted down and killed as soon as possible.

Sometimes, as they ranged, the pair met another wolf from the pack. Always he was coming from or going out to a hunt, and always the two sat quietly while he went about his family affairs. The pack must live, and it could survive only by reason of the squirming cubs which lay in the dens, helplessly dependent on the hunters.

Wherever else they journeyed the two went freely and arrogantly, caring for nothing and killing where and when they chose. And now a new mark of respect attended the black wolf; his bullet scar, previously a mark of shame, had become a badge of honor. There were deadly creatures in the wilderness, but none more to be dreaded than men. And though only a few of the forest's inhabitants had seen the bones of Alex Chirikov, those few seemed, in some mysterious way, to have passed the word along that a man lay dead among the spruces and that the black wolf had killed him. Now the forest creatures were very quiet when the black wolf came near; they knew he was supreme.

So the black leader and the one-eyed gray continued on their murderous, careless path, and even the grizzlies, which normally yielded the trail to nothing, moved aside to give them half the room. The black wolf looked at the grizzlies as he passed them, and drooped his tail as if to acknowledge their courtesy. He was not afraid of them, but he knew their iron strength, and that they would give battle to anything at all, including men, if they thought they had any reason to fight.

Down under the windfall, the big gray dog had been in desperate trouble for some days now. Since that late winter day when she had first heard her puppies mewling beside her, she had had two all-important problems: keeping them warm and feeding them. After the chinook dispersed the frigid cold and the spring sun sent its life-giving rays streaming into the wilderness, keeping the pups warm was a problem no longer. But in its place had come a new and much more serious difficulty.

As she hunted, she came to know every square inch of forest that was within immediate striking range of the windfall. She had travelled every rabbit run, lain in ambush beside every squirrel den, stalked every flock of grouse and spruce hens. She knew where the root-digging muskrats emerged from their watery haunts to find succulent bulbs along the bank, and the winding trails used by the spitting, musk-exuding mink when they travelled the creeks. Many times she had hunted at every one of these places, and at most of them she had taken game.

That game which was least alert and fleet of foot had been the first to fall. After she had skimmed off the easiest hunting, the gray dog worked harder and harder to get the next stratum. Now there remained only the fleet, the alert, and the strong. It was very difficult to get any food at all, without long trips from the nest; that meant the pups were left too long alone.

They were growing like thistles and, as they grew, they were finding the windfall in which they had been confined for so long much too small for their strengthening muscles and boundless energy. Now, instead of following her a few feet and returning to the nest, they trailed her to the very entrance of the den. A few days later they were piling out into the sunshine, and one morning began to follow her right into the forest.

The mother dog whirled and drove them back with punishing teeth that nipped without hurting their puppy-soft skin. Yelping indignantly, the two silver-gray pups fled back to the nest. Outraged, the masked-face puppy followed them a way and sat down to watch his mother disappear. The gray dog went openly into the forest, then turned and slunk back to hide behind a small spruce. In a few minutes she saw the steel-gray puppy leave the shelter, and on paws that now seemed too large for his body venture down to the little creek. He stood beside a quiet pool, entranced by his own reflection in the water.

The mother dog rose nervously, half-minded to drive him back. The steel-gray puppy had been a problem from the very start, and with every day he was becoming more of one. He resented punishment instead of being cowed by it, and as soon as he thought his mother was out of sight he did as he pleased.

Queen turned and went into the forest; she knew there was no use in chasing the puppy back. But with every step she travelled a gnawing anxiety travelled beside her.

She crouched beside a rabbit run in a thick growth of willows, her head on her paws and her plumed tail outstretched. Big feet silent on the packed run, wobbling its inquisitive nose, a snowshoe rabbit that had donned its summer coat of brown came into sight. The big gray dog crouched lower, trying not to breathe, as she sought to hide herself in the earth. Just at that moment a vagrant breeze from the windfall touched her nose. Anxiously she rose to test the story that breeze carried.

For a split second the rabbit stood galvanized into frozen immobility. Then it gave a prodigious leap, landed with a thick clump of willows between itself and the gray dog, and disappeared. Queen paid no attention to the rabbit, but whined deep in her throat. Instead of continuing her hunt, she trotted back to the windfall. She approached cautiously, quietly, again slinking up behind the little spruce tree and crouching where she could see without being seen.

All winter long a fat old porcupine had lived in a grove of birch trees just in front of the windfall. Happily grunting, gnawing the bark upon which he lived, and descending one tree only to make his ponderous way up another a few feet away, he had made his way, unmolested and unmolesting. Now at last, with the sharp tang of spring enlivening even his sluggish blood, he had come down from his birches to drink at the creek. He passed two big spruces that stood like sentries between the birches and the windfall, and had just started across a small clearing when the steel-gray pup saw him. At once the puppy ran eagerly forward to investigate this new friend.

When the gray dog came on the scene the puppy was racing around and around the porcupine, yapping at the top of his shrill voice, crouching with his head on his fore paws, wagging his tail furiously, and getting up to run again as, in every way he knew, he invited the grunting quill pig to frolic with him. The porcupine stopped his waddling way, trying with his dull brain to understand the noisy thing. He sniffled at some tender grass, and the bouncing puppy went around him again.

A dull, meek creature, the porcupine had no need to be anything else. He was sluggish and slow, but his weakness was protected by a thousand little needle-pointed barbed spears that stood ready to penetrate anything rash enough to touch him. Not wanting trouble, preferring to go his own placid way, the porcupine rattled his spears warningly at the puppy and chattered with his teeth. The puppy went into another paroxysm of wild joy. Around and around this enticing new friend he went, yapping at the top of his voice. Then he tripped on a stone, sprawled head over heels, and when he regained his feet his nose touched the porcupine's back.

With a single shrill yelp of mingled pain and astonishment, the puppy drew back and squatted

on his haunches. Bewilderedly he pawed at the
two quills that dangled from his nose, while he
looked in amazement at the false friend who had
so unjustly put them there. Because he was what
he was, the descendant of a fighting strain of dogs,
his next reaction was anger. A baby growl rattled
in his throat. Lifting his feet high into the air, ears
up and ruff bristling, he advanced on the porcupine.

Only then did the gray dog act. Leaping from
behind the spruce, she placed herself between the
puppy and the porcupine, and when he would
have gone past her she growled. Perplexed, the
masked-face puppy sat down again, watching the
porcupine resume his unhurried journey toward
the creek.

The puppy ran his tongue out, feeling the quills
in his nose and tasting the drop of blood that bubbled from the little wounds the quills had made.
He thrust his smarting nose against the grass, and
again fell to pawing at the quills. A sharp yelp
escaped him. He had unwittingly placed a ponderous front paw on one of the quills, recoiled
with the pain it caused, and pulled the quill out.

Meekly he followed the gray dog back under the
windfall, and while she lay there, feeding the two
silver-gray puppies that climbed eagerly about
her, he fell to pawing at the other quill. Again, to
the accompaniment of a shrill yelp of pain, he
stepped on it and accidently pulled it out. The
chastened puppy sat soberly down, every now and
then running a pink tongue over his sore nose.

As though she had made a sudden decision,
Queen rose and trotted out of the windfall. Their
meal interrupted, the silver-gray puppies tumbled
after her while the mask-face, still licking his sore
nose, followed in the rear. When she reached the

entrance to the windfall the big gray dog kept on instead of stopping, and not until she was a hundred feet or more from the den's entrance did the silver-gray puppies pause. Suddenly aware of the tremendous distance they had come from anything they knew, they looked back at the windfall, then squatted down, pink tongues hanging out excitedly. The steel-gray puppy made a sudden wild rush past them.

He had always wanted to go into the forest, and now that he could do so with official sanction his enthusiasm and joy knew no bounds. Clumsily he rushed at a red squirrel that stood six feet up on a spruce trunk, and stood under the squirrel, awakening the forest with his shrill yaps. Valiantly he tried to climb the tree, but fell over backward in a pile of soft spruce needles. Immediately he picked himself up and resumed his yapping.

The mother dog trotted back to the other two puppies and licked their faces. With coaxing little whines she lured them on, and they tumbled at her heels. When the masked-face pup started to run ahead, she nipped him back. Then she continued past all the hunting trails she had known so far.

A great peace of mind had suddenly descended on her. Her problems had been manifold, but now, magically, they were solved. She had not dared remain for long away from the windfall because of possible danger to the pups beneath it, and because she had had to hunt in the same places every day, hunting had been difficult. Now that she had the puppies with her she could protect them, and at the same time she could venture into better hunting grounds.

She led her brood over the dim forest trails to a wide meadow. A caribou cow and calf that were feeding in the meadow raised their heads to look at them. The silver-gray puppies sat beside their mother, shivering in the presence of beasts so large and strange. The mask-face trembled eagerly, rearing to place his front paws on a rock so he could see better. With a swift little run he tried again to go past his mother, but she nipped him back.

The gray dog led her three across the meadow to a stream. There were so many rabbits in the willows beside the stream that their reeking odor rose like a blanket above the willow roots. A big brown snowshoe leaped away, and the masked-face puppy gave yapping chase. Twenty feet away another rabbit thumped the earth, warning all the rest of danger that had come into the willows. Queen bounded after her errant son, and for the third time that morning chastised him. Subdued, but still wildly excited, he lay beside his brothers while the mother dog went alone into the willows. Five minutes later she was back with a snowshoe rabbit hanging limply from her jaws.

She laid it beside the pups, and backed away to watch their reactions. The two silver-gray puppies stood at a safe distance, craning their necks curiously and bending their heads toward the rabbit. The masked-face one advanced cautiously, and sniffled the dead rabbit while he tried to place in his own mind exactly what it was and why it was here. The rabbit smelled good. Flicking out a tentative tongue, he licked the brown fur. When his brothers would have approached, he warned them away with puppy growls. He seized the rabbit's ear and fell to dragging it about, until the rabbit rolled over a stone. Falling to one side, one of the big hind feet brushed against the puppy's cheek. His reaction was anger. Leaping at the rabbit, he buried his puppy teeth in it. A new, strange, and thrilling taste came to him, one he had never before experienced. He sat down, licking his own jaws. Again he leaped and sank his teeth in the rabbit.

His brothers advanced again, and when the mask-face tried to drive them off, the mother dog interfered. The three pups stood together, worrying the rabbit and pulling it apart.

Thus they learned the taste of meat.

Forty miles to the north, the black wolf and his freebooting gray companion pulled down a velvet-horned buck. The two feasted, then sought a bed near their kill and slept. There was no hurry; game was so plentiful that they scarcely had to seek it.

The two raised their heads as a pair of wolves from their pack led five cubs out to hunt. Quietly they lay down again. When winter came, the best and strongest of those cubs could join the pack. The rest would either be chased away to lesser packs or be killed.

After a while the pair of wolves went lazily down to drink. Summer time was leisure time and there was never any hurry or worry. If they travelled a mile a day, that was far enough. Winter, with all its struggles, would bring long trails and hard chases. They would rest while they could.

Still, day by day, they were moving ever nearer their home range on the Carney.

4. The Battle

June came to the wilderness, and one by one its golden days burst like bubbles over the vast reaches of spruce, the jackpine flats, the tangled alders, and the willows where the bull moose browsed.

The bulls were not now the strutting, mane-bristling creatures that would stride through the forest in fall, and battle each other for the favor of the cows in mighty tests of strength. Now their palmated antlers were still growing, and were covered with a sensitive fuzz that gleamed like brown velvet when the sun struck it. As they browsed, riding the willows down with their massive chests and eating the soft shoots that thus came within reach, the bulls were very careful not to bump their antlers or to injure them in any way. The males had strength in their heavy hooves, but their antlers were the real proof of their power and masculinity. Down to the least yearling, each bull was proud of them.

The cow moose kept their gangling, mule-like calves in the thickets, but both cows and calves came out to graze on the green carpet of grass that had sprung up wherever there was a gap in the trees. Or they ventured to the lakes and streams, closing the valves in their nostrils when they ducked their heads to pluck and eat succulent bulbs.

The caribou bulls, gathered in various herds, had gone far to the north, swimming lakes and fording rivers as they travelled to cooler places where there were fewer mosquitoes to plague them. The caribou cows, with their calves beside them, had also betaken themselves to their summer haunts.

Spruce hens and grouse clucked to their feathered broods as they led them to favorite feeding places. In their thickets, half-grown snowshoe rabbits gnawed new and venturesome runs beyond the places where their cautious elders went. Fox and wolf cubs came to the mouths of their hidden dens to soak up sunshine and gambol with their brothers and sisters. Myriads of tiny fish swam in the shallow parts of the lakes and rivers. There was scarcely a tree that did not hold a nest wherein baby birds gaped with open mouths while their parents engaged in a ceaseless hunt for more and still more food. Ducks, geese, and swans, back from the tropics in which they had passed the harsh winter, initiated their downy young into the mysteries of the things they must know if they were to live.

But if June was a time of bursting life it was also a period of swift and sudden death. Weasels whose racing bodies flashed like so many inches of running water prowled about looking for anything they could kill and eat. Fishers hunted food for their young. Marten slipped among the trees, and out from their hidden dens beneath the most secluded windfalls the wolverene mothers fared on an endless prowl for the food their gluttonous young demanded. Life bloomed everywhere, but the death without which no life would have been possible brushed its cold fingers into every nest, every den, and every hidden nook. Of all the wilderness creatures, only the grunting, head-swinging grizzly went happily on his way without a desperate urge to take another life or an equally desperate fear that he might have to give his own.

A terrible enemy when aroused, most of the time the grizzly was an amiable beast; his good nature sprang from the knowledge of his own formidable strength. He was not truculent because he had no need to be, and he asked no feast of warm, living flesh because he did not care for it. The grizzly was a gourmet who took only what he considered the tastiest and best. He knew where the tenderest bulbs and roots were to be found and, like the pig whose grunt he imitated, he dug them out and ate them. The myriad-swarming ants whose grubs he liked, or the locations of the bees' honey caches, were no mystery to him. The grizzly lived contentedly and peacefully, and when he did eat flesh it was usually from a wolf kill. The wolves might come back, and rage because their property had been violated, but even the most desperate wolf never undertook to punish a grizzly.

Most of all the grizzly liked fish, and just as he knew even the smallest secrets about that part of the forest through which he ranged, so did he know the favorite haunts of the big Dolly Varden trout that lay in sheltered pools. He understood, too, the times when those trout might choose to swim upriver to another pool and the grizzly was well aware that, when they travelled, their gleaming backs broke the surface of the shallow riffles which were their highways between pools.

This morning the grizzly was sitting in such a riffle, the rushing water beating at his brown rump. He sat absolutely still, while he kept his head cocked and his eyes fixed on the crystal-clear water that poured around his solid fore paws.

A few feet downstream there was something that might have been a shadow, only the grizzly knew that it was not. Unmoving, not even blinking, he kept his eyes on the twelve-pound trout that was starting to fight its way upstream through the swift riffle. The trout paused behind a stone that broke the riffle's force, then, rested, came on again.

Now the grizzly could see the trout, and through the clear water every detail of its body-wriggling, fin-propelled progress was plainly evident. It was a long trout, with an undershot lower jaw and vivid red coloring that accented the silver on its sides. The grizzly continued to remain perfectly still, while his tiny eyes followed the trout's every movement. It came nearer and nearer, and paused again as it viewed the unexpected dam formed by the bear's ample hind quarters. The trout gathered its strength for the swift rush that would carry it through the white water that eddied around the grizzly's paws. It darted forward.

With unbelievable speed for anything so big, the grizzly slapped once with the four-inch claws that tipped his ponderous fore paw. A geyser of water rose, and broke into a million sun-tinted bubbles through which, for a split second, a tiny rainbow shone. The big trout rose with the water, flying in a curving arc and landing on the slippery rocks beside the stream. As though it were still trying to swim, the trout bent and distorted its body in a series of swift convolutions that took it down the bank and nearer the water. The grizzly got up, and made ready to strike the trout again as soon as it had twisted itself back to the stream.

Then the willows beside the stream parted and the masked-face puppy came out. Without hesitation he pounced on the flopping fish, pinning it down with his paws and sinking his sharp teeth into its slippery sides. The puppy walked backward, dragging the trout up the bank toward the willows.

Down by the stream, the grizzly's astonishment turned to slow rage. With a little bawl of anger he scrambled up the bank. Then he stopped, pacified. The masked-face puppy, sensing the rage his act had inspired in the grizzly, had dropped the fish and retreated a respectful distance to one side.

He sat still, moving only the very tip of an appeasing tail, as he watched the bear come up to sniff at the gasping trout. The grizzly bit his catch in half, swallowed the part with the head still on, and turned to the other half. He severed that part just ahead of the tail, and left the tail lying on the bank of the stream. It was as though he offered a reward to the puppy for saving his catch; actually the grizzly did not like fish tails and never ate them. Finished with his meal, the grizzly ambled over to sniff at the masked-face puppy.

The puppy sat perfectly still, and out of the mazes of his brain recalled that incident of two months ago when this same bear had wandered in front of the windfall and he had licked its face. He had respected it then even as he respected it now, but he knew that he had nothing to fear from this amiable monster of the wilderness. He was right, for after looking him over, the grizzly ambled up the creek to a riffle where he might catch another trout. After the bear had gone the puppy gobbled up the fish tail, then started back into the spruce forest.

He stood a moment, one forefoot uplifted and his nostrils working as he strove to detect the elusive thread of scent left by the gray dog and the two silver-gray puppies with whom he had left the windfall nest early that morning. Now four months old and a quarter grown, the puppy was almost a miniature representation of what he would be when he had achieved his full growth. No longer with a tendency to flop and droop, his ears were sharply erect. The steel gray of his heavy coat had deepened and intensified, as had the black and white mask on his face. His tail was plumed, his body sturdy, with a powerful suggestion of growth to come. His staghound father and his crossbred mother had given him both size and weight, but his shape and grace—that of the Husky—he had drawn from his mother alone.

After a moment the puppy raced into the forest. He ran through a grove of closely growing spruces, down a slope, and splashed across the stream at its foot to climb another slope. The puppy's wild gallop slowed to a trot; his nose told him that his mother and brothers were just ahead. The steel-gray puppy halted, facing directly into the north wind until he knew exactly where they were. When he went on again, he trotted slowly.

At the confluence of two small creeks that flowed from separate valleys and met to form one large stream, he met his mother and brothers. The big gray dog was pawing something that was imbedded and half lost in drifting spruce needles. It was a mitten, an old woollen mitten whose threads had been ravelled by nest-building squirrels, and the puppy wrinkled his nose at the faint odor that still clung to that mitten. It seemed a familiar scent, but he could not remember it nor did he have it stored in that part of his brain wherein all scents were catalogued. The puppy sniffed at the mitten again, long and carefully, and filed the impression away in his brain. If he met that scent again he would know it.

Even though she could not read the crudely stitched "Link Stevens" that was still legible across the wrist protector, the gray dog knew who had lost that mitten. She whined excitedly, and held her nose to the north wind as though that might bring her some tangible evidence of the man she had once known.

Her tail stiffened suddenly, and the ruff on her neck bristled as she caught a scent that had nothing to do with Link Stevens. Summer-mild now instead of winter-harsh, the north wind still brought to every woods dweller the news of the travellers along the wild paths it crossed and what they were doing. A half-mile away from the gray dog and her pups, the wind had played over the backs of the black wolf and his fierce, one-eyed companion.

It carried the tale of their presence exactly as it was, as all the woodland dwellers knew it. There was cold fear in the story, and murmurings of unrestricted murder, and half-whispered little warnings of the way in which Alex Chirikov had died. The friendly north wind told everything to get out of the way, for the beast which was no longer a wolf but a werewolf was coming. The gray dog accepted that warning. Sitting beside his mother, trying to read and interpret the tale exactly as the big gray dog had, the masked-face puppy turned when she did. The silver-gray puppies crowded at their heels as they started up the hill.

Queen trotted faster, broke into a run, and

dodged onto one of the moose trails which was part of their regular highway when they came this far. One of the silver-gray puppies whined piteously, aware that terror was afoot in the wilderness but not knowing what it was. The mother dog mounted another hill, and trotted through the thick spruces on its sloping side to the old windfall in which her puppies had been born. It was the best and safest refuge she knew.

Outside the entrance, realizing that something cold and cruel was afoot, the silver-gray puppies whined and walked aimlessly about each other. The masked-face pup sat down, testing the wind and trying to interpret its message as his mother was doing. Wolf scent was heavier now; the wolves were nearer. Having found a dog belonging to man, the black wolf was on their trail.

The big gray dog turned suddenly, falling upon the pups with admonishing growls and sharp nips. Whining, sick with dread, the two smaller ones ran under the windfall and lay down in their old nest. The masked-face one went more slowly, looking back over his shoulder as he walked. He saw his mother take up a position at the entrance.

The steel-gray puppy sat down, curling his tail about his legs and looking toward the entrance. He was badly frightened, but the sense and courage which he had inherited from his ancestors overrode his fear. He had seen death, and had some conception of what it was, and why prudent creatures ran from it. He had also learned that when you could no longer run you must fight, and it was well to have some place from which to battle.

He walked slowly along the windfall's dark interior until he came to a small opening leading off to one side. He paused there, backing into the opening and testing it to see if there was enough room on either side for an enemy to slip through. There was not; the place was little larger than his own body. His back and sides protected, the masked-face puppy stood ready to meet whatever might come. He had done all his instinct could tell him to do.

When the wolves came, they did so even more silently than the wind that sighed over the wilderness without ruffling a single branch. First there was nothing. Then there were two apparitions among the spruces, two deadly things that walked lightly as fairies but breathed the kiss of death. Crouching in his tree, the red squirrel saw them. The whiskeyjack that flew away without uttering so much as a single cry saw them. The old and grizzled snowshoe rabbit hiding in his thicket saw them. The mother dog, standing silently in the windfall's entrance, saw them too.

The two wolves advanced side by side, the one-eyed gray to the left and the black monster to the right. There was no hurry. They would kill the gray dog—a creature of a hated man—but if they could help it they would not get hurt while killing. They paused a few feet from the gray dog, looking the field over with all the intelligence of military commanders.

The black wolf sat down on his haunches, running his tongue out while he looked over every inch of the embattled gray dog, probing her strength and her weakness. The wolf grinned fiendishly. The gray dog was ferocious, but the black wolf had seen ferocious creatures before, and the dog was holding her head just a little too high.

Legs stiff, tail straight behind him, the one-eyed wolf got up and stalked slowly forward. An inch, a half-inch at a time, his big paws moved. He tensed himself for the rush that would carry him forward to bowl the big dog over. Stiffening, he made his rush.

Only the gray dog was not where he thought she would be. Standing in the windfall's entrance, awaiting the battle she knew must come, she had studied her opponents even as they had studied her. The gray dog had been too long on the trails, and had fought too many battles, not to recognize and take advantage of any weakness in an enemy. The wolf rushed her exactly as a dog would have rushed, and as she had been attacked many times before. When he came she side-stepped, and drove in to strike at his most obvious weak spot.

It was a lightning encounter, a short intermingling of two gray bodies and eight shuffling feet. When it was over, the dog was back in the windfall's entrance, ready to repel again. But where the wolf's one good eye had been, there was now a bloody socket. Long fang marks traced a bleeding path down his cheek.

The wolf whimpered deep in his throat, and put his head to the earth while he brushed both paws down his pointed muzzle. He yelped shrilly, pushing his head farther into the dirt, and another helpless whimper rose in his throat. When he tried to run he bumped a tree, and recoiled in terror to brush against the black wolf. The blind wolf brought up short, whining as though pleading for help.

The black wolf understood strength and ferocity, but never pity and mercy. His razor-edged teeth slashed once, and again. For a moment the gray wolf stood on unsteady legs, then collapsed with a single strangled yelp. The blood from his ripped throat spilled in a hot, gurgling stream. The black wolf scratched dirt over his fallen companion and walked contemptuously away. For once in his life he had done a kindly act.

He sat down again, facing the snarling gray dog. When she made a short, swift rush the black wolf did not move. He knew that she dared not leave the entrance, and give him an opportunity to slip past her. She would not come out to him.

The wolf grinned wider, and there seemed to be a hint of approval in his eyes as he studied the gray dog. He understood and appreciated all the finesse of killing, and the gray dog had done exactly what he would have done in tearing out the gray wolf's good eye. If she had been a wolf, the black leader would have taken her for his mate.

But she was a dog, a creature of man, and therefore something with which the black wolf could never compromise. A thousand devils seemed to dance in his eyes; he had to kill this dog because of the hatred that consumed him. He knew the dog was trying to probe his weaknesses, but none knew better than he that he had none. The black wolf also knew how to bide his time, and he knew that time would come. He could hear the whimpering puppies within the windfall.

Not daring to take her eyes from the wolf, Queen backed a little nearer her young. Now her sides and back were shielded by the windfall. The black wolf edged nearer as his grin was replaced by a snarl. He had not counted on this; he wanted plenty of room in which to maneuver when he finally attacked. He sat for a moment deliberating the dog's next move.

If he were dealing with a normal beast, one that would fight coolly, he would expect it to find protection for everything except its slashing fangs. But he faced an excited dog whose nervousness was heightened a hundredfold by the fact that she had young to shield. He could depend upon her doing something foolish.

The black wolf made a swift little rush which he checked abruptly. As he had anticipated, the gray dog came to meet him. Crouching low to the earth, the black wolf slashed once. His fangs, that could hamstring even a big bull caribou, sought and found the dog's left front leg.

Almost in the same motion the black wolf leaped away. Queen's front leg dangled uselessly beneath her, but she did not go down. She stood defiantly on her three good legs, still facing the wolf and still ready to fight. Only now she was crippled, and the black wolf knew he could finish the battle at his leisure.

He went in again, swiftly and so low to the ground that he seemed to be only half his normal size. Pebbles flew, and little dust bombs burst beneath his paws as he came suddenly up. From the first the gray dog had been holding her head too high. The wolf slashed again: his jaws found that fragile flesh and skin that shield the throbbing jugular vein. The black wolf clamped his jaws tight, and his razor fangs went through the dog's throat. When the rushing blood had died away to a few drops, he let go and backed away. Before she died, with one desperate final effort, the big gray dog tried to throw herself forward and resume the battle for her puppies' lives. She saw the wolf through glazing eyes, and opened and closed her jaws once. The valiant effort fell a foot short.

Under the windfall, still backed in the opening he had found, the masked-face puppy saw the black wolf run past. He heard the baby snarls of his brothers, and two shrill yelps as the wolf's jaws snapped twice. Then he prepared to defend himself.

He heard the wolf padding back along the passageway, and smelled its fetid body as it stopped in front of the small opening. Its great black head was lowered; its gleaming eyes looked in at him. The black wolf thrust his muzzle within the opening, intending to seize the puppy and drag him out.

With fury born of fear and desperation, but backed by all the courage of the gray dog and the staghound who had been her mate, the puppy fell upon the black muzzle and scored it with his teeth. He fought as the Husky fights, slashing and leaping back. And, even now, he did not fight blindly. A dozen times his soft body was within an inch of the black wolf's questing jaws. A dozen times, twisting agilely, the puppy eluded those jaws. He continued to score with his baby teeth, and a moment later the black wolf withdrew his scratched and bleeding muzzle.

He sat in the passageway, and licked the seeping blood from his muzzle, while fury doubled the hate he felt toward all things that had to do with men. He was king, but he was being defied by a snarling mite whose back he could break without exerting a quarter of the strength in his jaws. Again he thrust in his muzzle, and again the furious puppy fell upon it, raking with his teeth and leaping back to slash again. The black wolf snarled in rage, and within his haven the puppy snarled back. Working his big paws rapidly, the black wolf started to enlarge the opening. The dirt-covered paws came within the puppy's reach, and he slashed at them, too. He was fully aware of the advantage of his position, and that the wolf could not reach him as long as he stayed there and fought.

The black wolf trotted to the windfall's entrance. For a full half-hour he remained there quietly, hoping the puppy would come out. But the friendly little breeze carried his scent to the mask-face, who had no intention of coming out. Strong within him was the will to survive, and only his cunning could help him.

Throwing caution and strategy to the winds, the black wolf raced down the passageway again. He thrust his muzzle within the opening once more, and tried to crowd his massive shoulders through. The puppy was not snarling now; he needed all his breath for fighting. Backing to the end of his retreat, where he was scarcely an inch from the farthest point the wolf's jaws could reach, he slashed and ripped with his puppy fangs. Courageously, guided by instinctive knowledge of what he should do, he struck again and again. Once he got a mouthful of black hair, and tasted wolf blood on his tongue and jowls.

When the black wolf abandoned the attack this time, he knew the weakness of his own position and the strength of the puppy's. He also knew how to wait. For two days, visiting the windfall often, he stayed and hunted nearby.

But it was the third day before the puppy came out.

5. Hunger

When the masked-face puppy finally came out of his hiding place, he did so slowly, warily, not exposing himself until he was sure of what was before him. He was very hungry, and had a raging thirst, but even stronger than the demands of his belly was the instinct of self-preservation. He crept out cautiously, every sense alert, and peered up and down the passageway under the windfall. Nothing stirred. He sat down and scratched an ear grimy with the dirt that for three days had been his bed. But even as he did so, he remained watchful for the return of the black wolf.

Involuntarily the puppy snapped at a big blue fly that buzzed near, then glanced quickly toward the mouth of the windfall. Out there a stick had cracked, and he did not know why it had. He sniffled carefully, caught only the odors of the dead things that lay at the mouth of the windfall, and dismissed the noise as something of no consequence. Already he had learned to depend on his nose as his main sense. If his nose could not verify the existence of something nearby then that thing did not exist.

The puppy went three feet from his hiding

place, and again sat down ready to dash back into it the second danger threatened. A growing loneliness came over him; he whined pleadingly and the end of his tail wagged as though he expected his mother to answer the plea. Nothing came.

He ventured on toward the littered nest in which he had been born. His nose told him that his two brothers were there, but there was something about their scent, something cold and fear-inspiring, that had never been evident before. The puppy's ruff bristled; he walked a step at a time, ready at any second to fight or run. Advancing cautiously, he came to where he could see the windfall nest.

The two silver-gray puppies lay where they had fallen. Stiffly outstretched, their lips were drawn back in a perpetual snarl from baby mouths that would never open again. The wide-eyed puppy advanced tremblingly, and thrust his nose as far out as he could to sniffle at his dead brothers. Then, in sudden panic, he turned and galloped as fast as he could to the windfall's entrance. He sat there, ruff still bristled and, for the moment, afraid to go farther.

Just in front of the entrance, the one-eyed wolf lay where he had been cut down by his black running mate. The wolf's legs were extended, as though even in death he would like to run from the treacherous companion who had killed him. The red blood that had gushed down his neck was now only a rusty brown stain. The puppy looked, and sniffed, and cocked his ear to catch anything there might be to hear. A tiny growl rose in his throat. Wolves had come, and they had killed, so from now on they must be regarded as the deadliest of enemies.

The puppy shuffled his feet nervously, and

looked past the dead wolf at his dead mother. She lay to one side and ahead of the one-eyed wolf, still in the place where she had died in a hopeless attempt to defend the babies under the windfall. The puppy whined dolefully at her, and begged her with pleading eyes to get up and come to his aid. When she did not move the puppy looked suspiciously at the one-eyed wolf, and back at his mother again.

Then, crowding as close as he could get to that side of the windfall which was farthest from the dead wolf, he began to creep by. In a sudden little rush he was past, and out in the warm summer's sun. The puppy whirled to meet the one-eyed wolf in case it had arisen to follow him. He studied the dead wolf intently, and when it did not get up the puppy finally decided that it could not. Very slowly he walked to the body of his mother.

He lay down in front of her, and let his warm tongue run lightly over her cheeks. Then he slapped at her nose with his paw, and retreated a step, his pink tongue hanging from open jaws. When the gray dog did not move he drew back, puzzled. Then the dreadful certainty that his mother would never move again burst upon him.

The puppy sat down, curling his gray tail around his front paws and pointing his muzzle to the sky. The very tip of his mouth formed an anguished "o" as he wailed his heart-broken grief to the wilderness about him. But only the old porcupine, who had gone back to his birches, and a whiskeyjack that teetered on a limb of one of the spruce trees, heard him. The porcupine looked sluggishly around, and chattered his teeth because an unnecessary noise had arisen to break his pleasant slumber. The whiskeyjack laughed as only a jay can, chuckling mirthlessly to himself as if he enjoyed the troubles of others.

As suddenly as he had started, the puppy stopped his wailing. Very deliberately he walked back to his slain mother, and carefully sniffed her all over. Then he ducked under the windfall to sniff at his two brothers. For several minutes he stopped at the refuge from which he had successfully battled the black wolf. The second time he emerged from the windfall, there was within him something as deeply rooted as the arteries that carried blood to his own heart.

It was the scent of the black wolf, the pitiless murderer who had brought all this desolation. The puppy would know that scent whenever and wherever he met it; it marked the black wolf as individually as the finger prints of a human being marked a man. There could be a thousand wolves in the wilderness, but the puppy would know the black one from every pack mate. Furthermore, so keen were those senses which gave the puppy his olfactory powers, he would single out and know that scent instantly. It had become a part of him.

Something else was also stamped into the puppy's brain as indelibly as the black wolf's scent. For from the moment he had realized his mother was dead, there was born in the puppy a hate as undying, as unyielding, and as savage, as that which the black wolf himself felt for men and all things belonging to men. In his slaying, the wolf had at last created a deadly enemy, and one that for all his youth, was not afraid of him.

The puppy did not again look at the windfall. He walked straight down the slope toward the stream, beneath the whiskeyjack in his spruce, past the porcupine in his birches. Beside the stream, the puppy looked all around before bending his head to drink, and tested every breeze with his nose. Ten feet up the stream bank, under a snag of root which still supported a lightning-blasted tree, he scented a snarling mink and its fresh-caught muskrat. There was nothing at all in the opposite direction except a few companionable chickadees that chirped an invitation to become one of their friendly and peaceful band.

The puppy put both front paws in the water. His own masked face stared back at him as he thirstily lapped up a drink. He raised his head, letting the water that clung to the fur about his mouth dribble back into the stream, then he drank again. Still a third time he bent his head to lap up water, and the mink under the snag grew more furious because he did not go away.

His thirst satisfied, the puppy took his feet out of the water and stood on the stream bank. Again a surge of loneliness swept over him; he was beginning to realize how utterly desolate and helpless he had been left. It had always been sheer delight to accompany his mother on her hunting trips but, though the puppy always considered himself a creature of great hunting prowess, he had never actually caught anything. Now he was wholly at a loss as to how he should go about finding food.

He knew, of course, where the mink was and what it was doing. The puppy had never liked a mink's musk-scented self, but the warm smell of the freshly killed muskrat drifted enticingly out to him. Lacking definite knowledge as to just what he was going to do, the puppy trotted toward the snag.

Snarling, spitting, ruffled fur making it appear twice as large as it actually was, the mink rushed out at him. It stopped, a bare five feet in front of the puppy, and spat all the epithets of which a mink is capable. The puppy stopped interestedly, wriggling his nose, then took another step forward. Knowing that his bluff had failed, the mink darted back under the snag. Making sure he had another way out, just in case the puppy was able to get beneath the snag, the mink stood snarling over the prey he had captured.

Thrusting his nose against the snag, the puppy sniffed long and wistfully at the hot meal awaiting beneath. He splashed up the stream and around the snag to its other side, but again his questing nose encountered only a closely interlaced network of roots. Experimentally the puppy began to dig, and for a moment progressed nicely as his strong paws scraped away the thin layer of topsoil that the rushing stream had deposited beside the snag. Then he struck bed rock.

The puppy stopped digging, and went five feet upstream to sit with his tail around his front paws and his head cocked to one side as he studied all possible means of getting beneath the snag. There was meat under there, he craved meat desperately, and it was puzzling as to why he could not get it. But he could not.

The puppy left the mink to his dinner, and wandered disconsolately up the stream's side. The steep bank broke where a tiny stream purred into the larger one, and still with no idea of where he was going or what he was going to do, the puppy wandered up the rill. He found himself back in the spruce forest. Suddenly, startlingly, a big snowshoe rabbit darted away from him.

Without even a momentary thought as to whether he should, the puppy gave instant, violent chase. The snowshoe easily outdistanced him, and disappeared in some ground-hugging evergreens. Eagerly, wildly, the puppy panted up to where he had last seen the rabbit and cast about there. Very plain on the ground, the rabbit's hot scent came up to tickle his nose and set him drooling. Painfully, step by step, the puppy traced that scent to a worn rabbit run. With all the startling suddenness of the first, another snowshoe dashed away from him.

Again, and with no more thought for the tracks he had been following, the puppy gave instant chase. A second time the big hare ran easily away from him. The puppy sat down, panting hard, his pink tongue hanging out to its very tip.

This was a good game, as well as serious business. As soon as he had solved the mystery of the big snowshoes' swift and sudden disappearance, the puppy was positive he could catch one. Again a rabbit got up, and again the puppy had a wild but futile chase. The streak of stubbornness which had been inherited in such large measure from his staghound father was fully aroused now.

Rabbits could run. But so could he, and he was more than ever convinced that, if only he kept trying, he would be sure to catch one. Again and again he ran, always failing. With the late summer's twilight he went back near the stream.

There the puppy sat down, hungrier than ever, and suddenly acutely aware that, although the day could bring loneliness, the night could intensify that loneliness a thousandfold. Very cautiously he went down to drink, and just as quietly, trying to make himself small, he crawled up the bank to a bed of thick ferns. The hunting cry of a great horned owl drifted over the wilderness, and the puppy crouched with his head on his paws. He closed his eyes tightly, finding some comfort. It helped if he couldn't see anything.

He had heard owls cry a hundred times, but always before he had been in the company of the big gray dog. Sure that she was the most powerful creature in this or any other wilderness, the puppy would have paid no heed to a thousand owls as long as she was near. Now he felt very forsaken and alone, and tried to bury himself deeper in the depths of the ferns. Nearby a mouse squeaked, and the puppy winced. When nothing came he settled back in his bed.

Trembling, nervous, wholly alone in a world that seemed a thousand times as big as it had been before, the puppy shivered through the medley of squawks, shrieks, yells, rustles, moans, and howls that mark a wilderness night. When the red sun climbed over the eastern horizon he arose gratefully, his fears almost forgotten. But he was terribly hungry.

Perplexed, he looked at the stream and back into the forest. Everything except himself seemed to be happy and well fed. The puppy whined anxiously, then struck out through the forest, away from the stream. He looked carefully at everything he saw, including the squirrels in the trees and the saucy whiskeyjacks that still laughed at him. No matter how small, if anything could be eaten he needed it. He leaped at a whiskeyjack that came to a low branch near him, then sat disappointedly while the bird sprang away, screaming its outrage. The puppy went on to a small clearing.

Set like a jewel in the forest, the clearing was about a hundred feet wide by two hundred long. Grass of purest green grew lushly all over, and dainty yellow buttercups nodded their fairy heads above the grass. The puppy sat down, peering around a tree at a moose calf which, with obvious relish, was cropping the grass.

The puppy knew that he could not pull down so huge a beast, but the calf seemed, somehow, to be getting something to eat. The puppy walked around the tree, standing a moment with tail wagging to show that he came in peace. The calf raised a head to look, even though it continued to chew the mouthful of grass it had plucked. Still demonstrating in every way he could that he meant no harm, the puppy advanced toward the calf. Even if it couldn't show him anything to eat, the calf might be a friend, and the puppy was sorely in need of one.

Suddenly there was a blasting snort, and from the trees beside the calf came a monstrous thing that seemed the very incarnation of fury. Eyes blazing and mane bristled, the calf's mother was thundering like an avalanche straight at the puppy. With a surprised little yelp he turned and fled.

Behind him, as he raced through the spruces, he heard the thudding hooves of the enraged cow, and the crackling of the trees and brush as she smashed through them. Intent only on escaping this terror, the puppy was not aware when the cow turned and went back to her baby. When the puppy stopped running, he found that he had once more come to the creek.

Here the stream banks were grassy and gently sloping instead of steep and rockbound, and between them the creek wandered over a series of riffles through shallow pools. The rocks found in the lower stream had given way to a thick coating of silt, and big Dolly Varden trout swarmed by the dozen in the placid pools. The puppy was attracted by a splashing, and turned his eyes toward it.

Dissatisfied with its pool, one of the big trout

had started upstream to another. Now its back fin and half its back broke the water as it fought upstream through the riffle. The trout rested a moment, and when it stopped it sank far enough into the silt so that only the very top of its back protruded above the surface.

The puppy leaped wildly and recklessly, and landed squarely in the creek, about four feet behind the trout. Disturbed by the commotion, the big fish threshed and wriggled as it strove desperately to reach the safety of deeper water. Eagerly the puppy bounded after. He gave a great leap, landing with all four paws straddling the trout while he sank his teeth into it. Fury broke out in the riffle.

The trout was a big one, with all the fierce strength of full growth, and when it began to struggle the puppy was carried with it into the water. His eyes and nose went under; his nostrils filled with water. Choking and sputtering, but holding fast to the fish he had captured, the puppy tried to brace his paws in the soft bottom. Again he went over, with the trout rolling on top of him, and still he held on. The desperate need for food lent strength to the puppy's jaws and stiffened his determination. Then, in a series of wild plunges, the trout hurled itself into the very shallow water near the stream bank. For a moment, exhausted, the big fish lay quietly.

A moment was all the puppy needed. He scrambled from the creek and braced his paws on the firm bank. His jaws were still fastened in the trout, which again started its wild struggling. The puppy closed his eyes while, inch by inch, he dragged his booty out of the water. Bedraggled, soaking wet, mud-spattered, he stood over his catch and looked proudly around. He had made his first kill. When the trout began to throw itself about on the bank, the puppy pounced on it and held it down.

At a slight noise from the top of the bank, the puppy looked around. The snarl that rose in his throat died there; he wagged a happy tail. Grunting, panting, and swinging his massive head, the huge grizzly was just behind him. But the grizzly only looked at him; if he would not relinquish his own catches, neither would he pirate anyone else's. The bear resumed his ponderous way up the creek, while the puppy lay down and feasted on fresh trout. When he had eaten as much as he could he dragged the rest of the trout up on the bank and hid it in some thick brush. The next morning he ate again, and that finished the trout.

The next day he encountered an otter on the bank, standing over a two-pound trout it had just caught. As the puppy rushed forward, the otter slid into the water and raised his sleek head to watch the puppy feed. But even as he ate, deep within the puppy's brain remained the thought of the fat snowshoes on their eternal runs; he was still determined to catch one.

Several times a day he would leave the creek and go into the forest, snuffling about the enticing runs and giving wild chase every time he flushed a rabbit. Invariably he failed to catch one, and was forced to return to the creek and the indifferent fare it offered.

Again he met the grizzly, standing in a shallow pool and slapping the big trout out with his paws. When the grizzly had caught enough, he went to dine on them. This time the puppy waited respectfully until he had finished, then gathered up and ate the tails. Twice more he caught trout of his own, and at various times he was lucky enough to frighten mink or otter away from fish they had caught. Slowly he worked his way up to where the stream narrowed down to a mere trickle.

He stood there, looking alternately at the very shallow water in which only fingerlings lived and down in the direction from which he had come. On sudden impulse he continued up, past the place where the stream was only a clear spring at the foot of a hill. The puppy climbed up the narrow, rock-strewn defile leading to the top of the hill.

He found himself in a gorge, a hundred feet long and with sheer rock walls that rose from ten to thirty feet on either side. The gorge was very narrow, and had a dank, cold smell. The puppy distrusted it, warned by instinct that it would be very easy to become trapped in there. If both ends were closed, anything in the center could not possibly get out. The puppy turned and went back down to the stream.

He wandered down its course as he had wandered up, eating what he could find and taking what he could from others that had been more fortunate in their hunting. As the weeks progressed he became thinner, but added to his length and height. No longer was he a fumbling, lost baby who feared noises in the dark. The puppy was fast learning to take care of himself, and he was more than ever determined to catch a rabbit.

One hot day he went into the forest for his usual rabbit hunt, and chased but failed to catch a half dozen of the big-footed hares that leaped up before him. Panting, breathless, and hot, the puppy drank from an ice-cold little spring whose waters trickled away toward the creek, then lay down beneath some cool spruce boughs whose feathered tips almost brushed the ground. He wanted only to rest, but presently, miraculously, there was a big brown snowshoe rabbit within inches of his nose. Incautious, unaware of an enemy about, the nose-wobbling rabbit hopped on.

The puppy acted solely on those hair-trigger nerves and instincts which were his by right of birth, and which had already been developed to a fine point by life in the wilderness. He leaped, and luck remained on his side. Taken by surprise, the rabbit moved too slowly.

Lifting his game aloft, the puppy looked all about, as though the entire wilderness should be a witness to his mighty deed. He had slain his first warm-blooded game. Certainly now he had a right to think of himself as king of the hunters. For a while, before he ate, the puppy permitted the rabbit to lie on the ground while he looked at it in unbounded admiration.

And he had learned an invaluable lesson. Snow-shoe rabbits were fast, but if it was impossible to catch them it was not impossible to ambush them. Thus the puppy added rabbit, the principal food of every meat-eating animal in the wilderness, to his diet.

Then one day, lying in wait beside a rabbit run, he made his split-second rush a moment too late. The startled rabbit raced away, with the puppy in close pursuit. But this time, instead of the rabbit's lengthening the distance between them, the puppy closed the gap. He came upon his fleeing quarry, and plucked it in mid-jump.

The flashing speed of his staghound ancestors was coming into its own. He was growing up.

6. The Trap Line

The little town of Masland had grown up around the railroad, and outwardly looked like any other small town along the line. It had pleasant homes, stores, a church, a school, and residents who for the most part worked at conventional jobs on the railroad or in the local pulp mill. But there was a certain air about Masland that prevented it from being just another whistle stop. For hundreds of miles to the west and north, and dozens of miles to the south, Masland was hemmed in by brooding wilderness over which many men had flown in planes but in which few had set foot.

Those few were the restless skimming of a multitude, the men who, even though they could see streamlined trains whistling down the line, and streamlined planes flying overhead, enjoyed neither of them, but plodded along on foot with an unquenchable curiosity to see what lay over the next enticing hill. They were the trappers who visited the town at intervals, and knew the surrounding wilderness almost as well as did its wild inhabitants.

Old Pete Roberts kept the biggest store in Masland, and outfitted most of the trappers. If they had a bad year, Pete staked them, and they paid him back whenever they could. If they had a good year, they spent lavishly. No trapper ever cheated Pete, nor he them.

Pete was leaning over the counter of his store, looking out at the dusty, idle street, when his eye was caught by a tall young man driving three laden pack horses. In his right hand he held the leashes of four big trail dogs; town dogs whose muscles were soft would stand no chance whatever against those husky brutes. Pete peered over his glasses for a better look. Sure enough, the man was Link Stevens, a youngster who went farther than anybody else into the wilderness and stayed longer.

Link tied the dogs to the railing in front of the store, then caught the trailing halter ropes of the horses and tied them. He entered the store.

"Hi, Link," said Pete Roberts, as casually as though he had last greeted the young man only yesterday instead of last summer.

"Hi."

"I see you're shy a dog."

"Yeah. That big Queen I got from Frenchy DuMont was with pups when I bought her. She ran off at the Carney. Trailed her for three days, then caught a blizzard and had to give up. Best dog I ever had, too."

"Tough luck. Probably got wolf-et. By the way, ever run across the black devil wolf that's supposed to hang out there, the one that killed Alex Chirikov?"

Link shrugged. "There's lots of black wolves, and they're all devils. But I never believed that story about Chirikov."

"Well, mebbe not, but that's what they say. What fur you got?"

"Lynx, marten, and beaver, mostly."

"You'd have got more for your lynx pelts if you'd brought 'em in a month earlier. Now the lynx market's dropping off."

Link said nothing; Pete gave trappers a fair deal, and told the truth. He watched the old man begin to grade and sort the furs.

"What's new in Masland?" he asked.

"Oh, Uncle Joe Darcey broke his leg. Al Toland's kid, Johnny, joined the navy. Tom Linkman . . . ."

Link listened to the small, unimportant, everyday doings of people whom he knew well. That was the kind of news that never penetrated the bush and he was hungry for it. Finally Pete stopped talking and began to figure with a pencil. He looked up.

"It comes to $976.35, Link. Pretty good catch."

"Not bad. Fix me a grubstake, give me fifty dollars, and credit me with the rest."

"Want a Link Stevens grubstake? A sack of salt and a box of cartridges for your .300?"

Link grinned. He had gone trapping four years ago, when he was sixteen, and because he had wanted to travel fast and far, he had taken only his rifle and what he could carry on his back. That "Link Stevens grubstake" was now famous throughout the trapping country.

"Better go a little heavier than that," he said. "Make it fifty pounds of sugar, two hundred flour, fifty each of rice and beans, thirty of raisins, maybe thirty of dehydrated apricots and peaches. You know what I need: about six hundred pounds all told."

"Okay. Put your dogs in the barn and your hosses in the south pasture. When you goin' back?"

"Couple of days."

"Let's see. This is Tuesday. Your stuff will be ready Thursday morning."

"Fair enough, Pete. Thanks."

Link Stevens went out, took his four pack dogs to Pete's barn, turned his horses out to graze in Pete's pasture, and strolled slowly up Masland's single street, noticing the few changes that had taken place during his absence.

He stayed in Masland for two days, visiting friends who lived there and other trappers who had come in. Before sunrise the third morning he was back at the pasture.

With tossing heads and flying tails, his three horses galloped to the far end of the enclosure and turned to look suspiciously at him. Link muttered under his breath. Trail horses did not look like thoroughbreds, but they knew everything there was to know about their jobs—and that included knowing when they were supposed to go to work again.

Link went into the barn and saddled Pete's white riding horse, but as soon as he rode into the pasture the three were away again. Link quartered across, spurring his mount and trying to run the pack horses into a corner. But a half-hour passed before he caught and bridled the first one, and tied it to the pasture fence. By the time he caught the other two, the sun was well up. He strapped blankets and pack saddles on the horses, and led them to the store. He grinned to himself.

It was the old storekeeper's vociferous claim that anyone past seventy-five had earned the right to do as he pleased. If he wanted to go fishing or sleep until noon, he did so. This morning he was not up, and the store was closed. Link's grubstake lay on the porch. There was a note fastened to one of the packs: "Good luck. Pete"

Link picked up a pack box, placed it on the saddle of one of the quieter horses, and tied it with the thirty-foot basket rope. He placed a corresponding box on the other side of the horse, laid the top pack across the panniers and the horse's back, and threaded the basket rope around them in such a fashion that everything was held in place. Then he laid a tarpaulin over the pack, and laced the whole thing down with a diamond hitch. Critically he inspected his work. A diamond hitch would hold a pack in place even if a horse bucked all over the trail, but it had to be thrown correctly.

He packed another horse in similar fashion, then cautiously approached the third, a blue roan that had as many tricks as a professional magician. But this morning, evidently, he was going to be good, for he looked calmly around, standing quietly while the first pack box was adjusted. Link put the other one on, and laid the top pack. Then, just as he was about to cover the load with a tarpaulin, the horse pretended to spook.

He neighed, and reared to paw the air with flying hooves. Held only by the basket rope, the top pack flew into the street and scattered its contents. The horse reared again. Already strained, the halter rope snapped, and the horse went bucking down the street. The side boxes flew off, scattering the various objects with which they were packed. Link stood grimly, watching the horse's wild plunges. Then a man rushed out to grasp the roan's halter rope. Link recognized Johnny Vanter, a trapper whose lines lay southeast of the Gander. Link walked down and retrieved the subdued roan's shortened halter rope.

"Thanks, Johnny," he said gratefully.

The other man grinned sympathetically. "That's a right disputatious hoss you got there."

"Yeah, but he'll get over it on the trail."

Link led the roan back to Pete's store, re-tied it, and picked up a club. He brandished it ostentatiously in front of the horse, which looked at him meekly. Link set about gathering up and repacking his belongings, but before he tried to put anything back on the horse he brandished the club a second time. The horse stood quietly, knowing what could happen if he did not. Then Link went to Pete's barn for his dogs, and headed out of town.

As soon as he was beyond the last house, he unsnapped the dogs' leashes. They bounded forward, sniffling eagerly at the rabbit runs they came across. Led by the fractious roan, the pack horses tried to crowd after the dogs, but were held back by Link's firm grip on their halter ropes.

Link made his camp that night where the snarling Cumber River raced between spruce-laden banks. He unpacked the horses, hobbling them and turning them loose in the grassy meadows that broke the forest on the Cumber's bank. He spread his sleeping bag, then cut a willow rod. Rigging it with a line, leader, and fly, he walked down to the Cumber, with the four dogs as eager spectators.

He cast his fly into a quiet bit of water behind a rock. Almost at once the line tightened, started across the river, and Link played a two-pound grayling in to the bank. He cast again in the same place; where there was one grayling there would be more. Twenty minutes later, with enough fish to feed the dogs and himself, he cooked his supper over an open fire beside the river.

At daylight the next morning he caught and packed the horses and led them half a mile upstream. Quieted here by level land, the Cumber did not snarl so furiously nor rush so fast. Link chivvied the horses into the water, and waded beside them. The dogs swam across.

From there on the trail was entirely through muskeg, with numerous squaw bridges—four eight-inch poles laid side by side—over the deeper holes. Alders and a twisted jungle of small spruces marked both sides, and made it almost impossible for a horse to stray. Nevertheless, the roan horse bogged down.

One second he was plunging through knee-deep muskeg. The next, he was mired almost to the bottom of his pack. The horse bucked and twisted, trying to find a foothold, but succeeded only in miring himself more deeply. Link cut a spruce tree, letting it fall over the muck and beside the mired horse. Patiently, carefully, he worked himself out on the fallen tree and unlaced the diamond hitch. He removed the top pack, then the side boxes, and carried them to the farther side of the muskeg. Relieved of its packs, the horse was able to free itself.

They went on, making time where the trail was good but slowing where it was bad. Fighting across rivers, through muskeg, and making their own trail where this one became impassable, they travelled farther and farther into the wilderness. The sixteenth day, two hundred and fifty miles from Masland, they came at last to the Gander.

Link's home cabin, a twelve by sixteen log structure equipped with heating and cook stove, and enough table and cooking ware for both Link and his infrequent guests, was on the north side of the river. Behind it was a storage shed, and to one side, separated far enough so their chained occupants could not fight, were five dog houses. On the river flat, fenced against raiding deer and rabbits by closely set saplings, was the vegetable garden that Link always planted as soon as the weather became warm enough.

He unpacked the horses and hobbled them in the rich meadows beside the Gander. Taking his rod down to the river, he caught enough grayling for the dogs, then started out with his rifle.

A doe with two spotted fawns ran before him, but he held his fire. A cow moose stalked awkwardly across a clearing, and farther on a velvet-horned bull stared suspiciously at him. Link half raised the rifle and lowered it again. It was too early in the season to shoot moose.

He stopped suddenly, his eyes attracted by a bit of color that was not just as it should be. It was a six-inch splash that showed through the laced branches of a tree, and did not harmonize with the summer colors. Link whistled. When a small buck started running through the trees, he shot, and the buck fell heavily. He dressed the little deer, shouldered it, and carried it back to the home cabin. He had meat.

Now there was endless work distributing supplies among his various out cabins, renewing trap-lines, cutting overgrown trails, preparing scents. Then one day the north wind carried snow on its back, and along its quiet edges the Gander formed a thin sheathing of ice. South-bound geese and ducks flew ceaselessly overhead. Rutting bucks with swollen necks strutted truculently around the low hills. Solitary moose grunted in their thickets. But Link waited. He wanted to get a moose, but animals in the rut are not the best eating.

One evening two weeks later, he had just stepped out of the cabin to drain a pot of potatoes when he saw what at first seemed to be a pack horse with panniers on the side, coming toward him. Then, as Link squinted into the gathering darkness, it seemed to have a rider with white chaps. The thing came nearer, and he saw that it was a big bull moose that had been scraping its antlers in the snow. It had been holding its head down, and thus achieved the effect of a horse and rider.

Link stepped back to get his rifle, squinted over the sights, and squeezed the trigger. A tongue of flame licked the darkness, and the bull took a few halting steps. It stopped, then settled slowly down. Link lowered his rifle with satisfaction; he had a good supply of meat for some time to come, and all was well on the Gander.

Two days later, while he was walking up a ridge, the snowshoe rabbit that ran before him showed purest white instead of brown or pinto. When the snowshoes turned white, other furs would be prime. It was time to set his traps.

7. The Race

During the summer the masked-faced dog grew
like one of the weeds that found rooting in the rich
silt piled up along the creek bank. Carried now in a
half-curve over his back, his tail was feathered
with fur as long and silky as that rich pelage which
covered the rest of his body. His chest was broad
and deep, his legs powerful, but trim like those of a
staghound. Lightly paunched, his flanks sloped
gracefully to well-muscled haunches. His big
head was tipped with pointed ears that no longer
drooped, and most of the puppy teeth in his powerful jaws had given way to the polished fangs of
maturity. He weighed more than a hundred
pounds, and the only puppyish air about him now
was a certain looseness of skin that foretold still
more growth to come.

He looked like a very large Husky, but was not a
perfect representation of one. The various breeds
in his ancestry had each bequeathed something,
but it seemed that he had inherited only the best
and most outstanding qualities. There was no sign
of weakness.

And, even as he had grown, so had he learned.
No longer was his hunting success dependent

upon sheer, blind luck; when he wished to eat he no longer had to take what offered or hope to rob a more fortunate hunter.

He knew all the rabbit runs for many miles around, and the best hiding places along those runs. But now he ambushed rabbits only when he was lazy or not especially hungry. Other times he simply ran them down; his staghound legs made it unnecessary to call stealth into play. It was enough merely to amble through a place where the snow-shoes were plentiful. Hearing him, the rabbits would freeze in their beds. As soon as he came close enough, they dashed madly away and be-trayed themselves.

But in the course of his other hunting the big dog had learned the value of both stealth and patience. Throughout his wild career he had slowly been assimilating such knowledge, and its value was driven home to him one hot day when he lay doz-ing in a small spruce grove.

He had eaten early that morning, and now wanted only to sleep before he went on another hunt. He had chosen the small spruces because they were shady, and because a series of small icy springs rising under the trees kept them cool. The busy little red squirrels who always seemed either to be cutting spruce cones or racing among their many hiding places had hushed when he entered the grove.

The dog's keen nose told him not only that there were squirrels in the spruces, but also how many there were and where they kept themselves hid-den. Well fed, he was not particularly interested in them. Sleeping, but equipped with senses that never slept, he knew that only the squirrels and himself occupied the spruce grove. Then, unex-pectedly, something struck him on the nose.

Two months before he would have leaped up, bristling and alarmed, ready to run or fight. But those two months had taught him much. Scattered throughout the hunting territory he had taken for himself were a dozen favorite thickets and copses, and almost always he bedded in one or another of them. At first, when he lay asleep and another beast passed, the dog had fled if that beast seemed at all threatening. Gradually he had learned to lie still, and dozens of times he had seen at close range animals which had not seen him at all. Sometimes, when the wind had been in their favor, they had smelled him and been nervous because he was near. But since they did not know exactly where he was, the advantage had always been his. Thus the big dog had learned the practical side of never revealing his own presence.

Now, when the small object struck his nose, he merely opened his eyes and lay very still. The falling object was a spruce twig to which was attached half a dozen cones. Frozen into silence when the dog had entered the spruces, the squirrel that was cutting twigs had decided there could be no harm in a thing that lay so still so long, and now he was hard at work again cutting more twigs. They rained down thickly, several in the air at once, as the busy little creature in the tree continued to cut them. The squirrel leaped from one branch to another, and peered down at the sleeping dog. He descended to another limb, sitting there in tail-jerking nervousness, and chattered experimentally. When the dog still did not move, the squirrel scampered down the trunk and began to cut the cones from the twigs on the ground.

Paying no attention to the dog, the squirrel passed several times within a few inches of his muzzle. The dog followed his busy progress with alert eyes and nose, and knew that he might catch and eat the squirrel any time he chose. Only he was not hungry, and the big dog killed only when he wished to eat. But he had learned something new. From that time on, he varied his menu with squirrel.

Similarly, he had learned about the swarming trout that lay in deep pools but so often climbed the shallow riffles. Formerly the dog had trotted aimlessly along the bank of the little stream which had become one of his favorite haunts, and simply hoped to surprise a trout ascending the riffles. Now he knew that, if he concealed himself beside almost any pool, sooner or later one or more trout would decide to go on to the next pool. It might be hours before they did, but there were times when patience was the only virtue if wilderness dwellers hoped to eat.

Then arrived the day when the growing dog became aware of his own power, and of the respect inspired in most other wild things simply because he was what he was.

The first dusting of snow lay on the ground and powdered the thick-set branches of the spruce trees. Ruffling its feathers in one of those trees, a whiskeyjack croaked dismally, as though this first positive evidence of the winter soon to come was most depressing. From everywhere in the spruces came the crisp sound of twigs striking the earth, as the frantic squirrels, afraid they would not have enough to eat, started work early in the morning and stopped late at night. Then, off in the forest, a moose grunted.

It was a deep, blatting note that in itself seemed to contain only discord. Yet there was something hauntingly sweet about it, and lonely; something that spoke of the grunting bull's tender yearning for the mate he hoped to find. The bull's grunt was an indispensable note of that wilderness symphony that is never still, that continues twenty-four hours a day, and is made up of birds' songs, the wolf's howl, the death whispers and shrieks of all those things which must die so that others may live, the wind sighing through trees, water rippling, ice grinding, frost-tortured trees groaning, and so many other notes that no one will ever be able to classify all of them.

The big dog heard the bull grunt, and knew the sound for what it was. A cow answered, and from another point in the forest a second bull that had heard her grunted a reply. The first bull called again, and now there was no tenderness in the sound. He had heard his rival, and was telling him in angry tones to keep away from the cow or fight. The second bull grunted his intention to fight, and the two started toward each other with all the crashing, tree-bending racket that can be made only by two bull moose, each of whom knows that he is better than the other and can hardly wait to prove it.

The big dog continued quietly on his way toward his favorite little stream. Actually, he was travelling a moose path. But during the summer, while the cows had been occupied with their calves and the solitary bulls had stayed in seclusion while their antlers grew again, no moose had used it. It had been trod by nothing save the dog, an occasional fox or coyote, or the big grizzly. While he tolerated such trespass, the dog had come to regard this path as his own special property. Now, to his sudden surprise, he came face to face with the smaller bull.

It was as big as a good-sized horse, and the bull's bristling mane made it appear even bigger. Its

eyes blazed redly, and its lips were drawn back
from yellowed tushes. Even a grizzly bear is not
more dangerous or unpredictable than a moose in
the rutting season.

For a moment they stood gazing at each other,
the bull moose on its way to fight for the favor of a
cow, to pit its swelling strength against another
bull, and the dog whose only desire was to visit the
little stream. Without warning, the moose
charged.

He came like a locomotive, nine hundred
pounds of sound and fury, rushing at the dog with
his head high and his sharp front hooves ready to
grind into pulp this presumptuous thing that dared
dispute its passage. For a moment the dog instinctively recoiled. Then a sudden resentment rose
within him. This was his path, something which
he held by right of discovery. Other creatures had
been granted a right-of-way on it, but they had
passed swiftly and respectfully as they made their
way toward paths of their own. Now, even though
it was huge and ferocious, something that had no
right to do so was challenging the dog's property
rights. A snarl bubbled in his throat.

When the moose reached the spot where he had
been, the dog was no longer there. Sidestepping,
he drove in at the bull as it passed, and left a clean
row of fang marks on its leg. Acting on instinct
alone, the dog had tried to hamstring his adver-
sary. He had almost succeeded.

With startling speed for anything so massive, the
moose whirled. Swift as he was, the dog was
quicker. Like a cat he danced away, and leaped in
again to score the bull's hot flank. This time he had
tried a wolfish stroke, the belly slash that disem-
bowels an animal and leaves it helpless. And again
he had come within an ace of succeeding. The

grunting moose turned again, and for a second stood pawing the earth. The dog seized the initiative.

Feinting, he dodged just as the bull's palmated antlers glided like polished sword blades over the place where he had been. Instantly the dog was in, diving at the momentarily unprotected front leg and slashing it. The bull made a wild strike, and his heavy fore quarters bent very low as he tried to pin the dog down with his chest. Elusive as a breath of air, the dog was away again.

Suddenly the bull turned tail and fled back in the direction from which he had come.

The dog watched him go, a great black beast that one moment could be a dynamo of ferocious, destructive strength, and the next, due to some queer quirk within his own brain, a frightened thing that would run away from a creature scarcely a tenth his size. There came the questioning grunt of the other bull, who did not know where his rival had gone. Then, somewhat disappointedly, he went to claim the cow for which he would not now have to battle.

Trotting slowly, sniffing at the hot scent of the running moose, the dog went along the path to the rabbit run upon which he always turned off toward the stream. The north wind, that had been howling high above the trees, swooped suddenly down near the earth, bringing with it a blinding flurry of snow that left an ermine coat over the old snow already on the ground. The dog blinked into the snow, and bent his head. Although the wind buffeted him and plastered his heavy fur close against his body, he felt neither its force nor the cold that accompanied it. Beneath his outer fur was a heavy, closely matted inner coat that would keep him warm even when the sparkling cold was at its cruelest.

The dog crouched beneath a low-hanging bough, his eyes on the riffles that led upstream from the pool beneath him. But the back fin of no fish broke those riffles; there was no motion in the pool. For no explainable reason, the trout had gone downstream to deeper water. The dog got up, and went into the forest to catch a rabbit. Four deer moved in front of him, and he sat silently until they had passed. Never had he thought of deer, nor any of the larger animals, as a possible source of food. There was plenty of small game that was easy to get.

For a week the dog prowled the forest, eating when he felt hungry and sleeping when he was tired. The snow came down, piling itself deeper and deeper while the wind churned it into drifts. Every spruce and jackpine was laden with snow. The whiskeyjacks clung to their thickets, miserable themselves but seeming to chuckle over the plight of everything else that was just as forlorn. The squirrels were snug in their dens, living on the pine and spruce cones they had gathered with such labor. Accepting the coming of winter as they did everything else in their troubled lives, the big snowshoe rabbits padded more runs to wherever they could reach food. The wind howled ceaselessly, until one day it brought to the big gray dog the scent he had never forgotten.

He had just eaten, and was lying in a thicket beside the now-frozen stream when the scent brought by the wind made him sit bolt upright. For a moment, while he quested with his nose, he did not move. Then he crawled out of the thicket, sitting in the wind's full blast while he sought to verify the elusive thread of scent. It came again, and a snarl rippled from the dog's throat; he knew that the black wolf was once more leading his fierce pack out to hunt. He knew as certainly as though he had been with them exactly where that pack was and what it was doing.

Now there were seventeen of the forest-ranging freebooters, each in itself a lean and hungry menace. But none was so dangerous nor so savage as the black monster who led them on their pillaging path and brought terror to the entire wilderness. Spread out at hundred-yard intervals, the pack was ranging with the wind while each wolf engaged on a rabbit hunt of its own.

The dog growled and took a few steps forward, but even as he did so he was afraid. With overwhelming force there returned to him the memory of this murderer's visit to the windfall, and the havoc he had wrought there. And this time there were many wolves. Their scent was plainer now, and the dog knew that the course they were following would bring them close to where he had bedded. The dog growled again, his hatred of the black wolf battling with the fear that bade him run. Glancing backward, while the wind plastered his curved tail against his rump, the dog slipped over the steep bank to the little stream's frozen surface. He began to trot up the ice.

He stopped a half-mile away, and again climbed the stream bank to sit on a little promontory where he could read to best advantage the story carried to him by the wind. He knew when the wolves came to the place where he had bedded, and that they stopped there. No longer were they separate wolves, each looking for its own game, but a terrible striking force welded into one by the inexorable will of their leader. The dog smelled the hate plain in the black wolf's scent, and snarled back.

There was hatred within him, too, but it was tempered by both fear and prudence. Although he was within a half-mile of the thing he wished most to kill, he knew he was neither mature enough nor experienced enough to know how to proceed with that killing. The dog began to run.

His nose held high, so he could take full advantage of the tale the wind told him, he raced up the frozen stream bed. He could tell that his wonderful staghound's legs were keeping him ahead of the sixteen gray wolves, but the black leader was slowly creeping up.

Even while he fled, the natural intelligence with which the dog was so heavily endowed directed his flight. Clear to the gorge on the very top of the mountain, he knew every inch of the way. And, if a fight was inevitable, he who could choose the scene of that fight always had an advantage. The puppy remembered his other encounter with the black wolf, and how he had effectively slashed from a narrow refuge into which the wolf could not enter. Only this time there was no friendly refuge. He would have to choose an eminence, preferably one where his back and sides would be protected, and meet the wolf there, for he could not outrun him.

The dog came to a heavy drift and slowed down a little. He knew that his enemy had cut the distance between them by almost half, and that he was gaining fast. Furthermore, since the dog was breaking the trail, the wolf did not have to struggle through deep snow. Behind the leader, strung out in the order of their speed, came the other wolves.

Because he knew the black wolf was drawing up on him, the dog ran easily, without exerting all his speed. If he did that he would be tired and hot when he finally turned, and he needed to be as fresh as possible when he finally stood fang to fang. Also, he knew exactly the place from which he wanted to fight.

The narrow, rocky gorge that ran like a deep knife cut across the top of this hill would be ideal. There, should they rush him, he could take the pack one at a time, and have some protection for his own flanks and back while he fought. The dog emerged from the spruces beside the little creek and began to climb the treeless, rock-bound side of the hill. Here, except for a few places where snow had piled and drifted against boulders, the wind had swept most of the snow away.

The dog stopped deliberately and turned to look behind him. A hundred yards away the black wolf emerged from the trees, and strained forward like a black streak. He, too, knew all about that narrow gorge and why the dog wanted to reach it. The black wolf panted and whined like a puppy as he stretched his long legs in prodigious bounds.

The dog ran on. He had gauged his time well, and could find a place of his own choosing before the wolf caught him. He reached the gorge and appraised it in one fleeting glance.

The sweeping wind had brushed the gorge's mouth clean, but it had taken the snow that had lain there and piled it so high in the center of the gorge that the drift's apex came halfway to the top of the twenty-foot wall. Beyond, toward the other side of the gorge, the drift sloped to more bare, frozen rock. The dog backed into this space between the side wall and the drift, and braced himself. He had been afraid when he had first scented the pack. Fear still lay coldly upon him, but since he had to fight, he was ready. He was about to try conclusions with the only creature in the world that he wanted to kill for killing's sake alone.

The black wolf stopped a little way down the slope. The thousand devils in his eyes seemed to dance with unholy glee as he studied the dog. As usual when he fought, he was in no hurry, and had no intention of getting hurt himself. He examined the ground like a field commander. The wolf opened his mouth, as though laughing. The dog was holding his head too high, just as the big gray female had done. Dogs usually did that.

Scattered out, with the slowest behind, the sixteen gray wolves came up to range themselves in a semi-circle behind their leader. Tongues lolling and tails flat on the frozen ground, they awaited the battle to come. It was not their fight; it belonged strictly to their black leader. His alone was the supreme pleasure of killing dogs.

The black wolf advanced very slowly, padding silently toward the embattled dog. It was not going to be the sort of battle in which he could fully satisfy his genuine lust for fighting. Had the dog been older and more experienced, he might have put up a fine battle, a fight to test the black wolf's skill. But this dog was little more than a puppy.

Holding his own head high, fixing his yellow eyes squarely on the dog's, the black wolf continued to advance. It was an old ruse, and one that had proven itself many times: let the opponent believe you are trying to hold his eyes, then leap in to deliver a crippling blow. The dog braced himself more firmly to meet the black wolf's attack.

Then, for no reason of which the dog was immediately aware, the wolf retreated. He slunk twenty feet down the slope, and sat with his front feet braced and his black tail curled around his paws. Presently the dog heard the padding of heavy feet, and at almost the same moment the breezes that sighed back and forth in the gorge brought him the scent of the monster grizzly.

The grizzly had gone up through the gorge a week before and into the country on the other side, to feast on brook trout which swarmed up the small streams to spawn at this season. Then the snow had come, bringing a great lassitude to the bear, and a desire to settle down for his long winter's sleep in a favorite den on the Carney. Having in mind only that he must reach that den, the grizzly ambled up the slope and calmly walked through the deep drift in the gorge.

For the past quarter-mile his nose had told him that the dog and the wolves were there at the mouth. The grizzly cared neither one way nor the other. He knew the dog had always been a friendly creature who had never bothered him. The wolves might be different, but ten such packs could not stop the grizzly's going to the den upon which he had set his mind.

Therefore, when he reached the mouth of the gorge, the bear walked indifferently past the dog, his huge bulk all but filling the narrow opening. He bent his head toward the black wolf, as though inviting him on. The grizzly, too, knew an ideal defensive position; if he had to fight the wolf pack that fight would take place right here. Opening his cavernous mouth, the grizzly yawned prodigiously, and shuffled his monstrous front paws.

The black wolf turned regally, as though he had intended to do so all the time, and led his pack down into the forest.

Meanwhile, knowing that his rear was effectively protected, the dog hastily back-tracked the grizzly to the other end of the gorge. Hate of the black wolf was still seething within him, but fear was stronger. He would have fought the wolf had that been necessary, but he was grateful because he had not had to.

He slept that night in a thicket beside a frozen lake, and because he was a stranger in a strange land he slept uneasily. Nothing disturbed him, and the next morning he continued down the sloping valley in which he found himself, eating when he was hungry, then pushing on again. It was the third day afterward when he came across the most puzzling trail he had ever encountered.

It was a very wide trail, which must have been made by something with monstrous feet. There was a faint scent connected with the tracks, and the dog remembered that he had smelled such an odor before. He sat down, puzzled. Having never seen one before, he could not know that this was a snowshoe trail. But he did know that the faint scent was the same one he had smelled on the mitten with "Link Stevens" stitched across the wrist protector.

Still puzzled, the dog followed the trail. Presently his nostrils were tickled by a most enticing odor, one that seemed to spring from the base of a small jackpine that stood a few yards off the trail. For a moment the dog stood still, his head high so he could analyse the scent more fully. Eagerly, his tail wagging, he trotted toward it. He stood over the very source of the scent, and thrust out an exploring paw to see if he could uncover it.

Suddenly some hidden thing which had betrayed no hint of its presence leaped out of the snow to grasp his right front paw. He was fast in one of "Link Stevens' " wolf traps.

8. The Captive

A mile and a half down the valley, while the four pack-laden dogs sat in the trail and waited for him, Link Stevens knelt to take a red fox out of a trap. Carefully he re-set the trap, and carried the fox out the same path he had used to come in from the trail. The four dogs crowded up to sniffle at it, then sat down in the snow, knowing they could rest until their master had pelted his catch.

Link skinned the fox, put the rolled pelt in his own pack, and cheerfully continued up the snow-shoe trail. He had been trapping for four years, but there had never been a better catch this early in the season. Almost every fur stretcher in his home cabin was decorated with a fox, coyote, or mink pelt, and there were already many cured pelts in his fur cache. He even had a few of the big timber wolf pelts, but not many. Aside from being bulky, and not worth a price in proportion to the space occupied by the pelts, wolves were hard to trap. They did not cling as closely to established runways as other fur-bearers did, and every trap in which a timber wolf was caught would be so fouled with wolf scent that it would be almost impossible to catch anything else in that trap. Most other animals feared timber wolves more than anything else.

Link whistled as he lifted one long, narrow snowshoe ahead of the other and strode up the packed trail. A trapper might operate for ten years, and not make expenses. Then he could have a really good year and make up for all ten poor ones. This was certainly going to be such a year.

There had been few storms and the snow was not as deep as it usually was at this time of year. The swarming snowshoe rabbits that were the basic food of every meat-eating animal were so plentiful that it was almost impossible to look anywhere without seeing one. Every fifty yards or so a fox, coyote, wolf, weasel or some other predatory animal or bird had killed a rabbit and left its unwanted remains on the snow, but there still seemed to be as many rabbits as ever. Meat had been no problem, since fifty moose and deer were wintering within easy range of Link's home cabin. Even as he was thinking of game, two moose ran up a small hill and stood looking at him. The four dogs glanced at the beasts, then returned to their eternal sniffling at rabbit tracks along the trail. Link grinned ruefully. All his dogs wanted to hunt was rabbits; he wished he had a work dog who was also a hunter.

Yuke crowded up to walk beside him and Link reached down to pat the big dog's head with his mittened hand. Yuke wagged his tail, and swung his muzzle to brush Link's leg. Then he stiffened, looking steadily up the trail. Tibby, Lud, and Kena, behind Yuke, crowded to the outer edges of the trail and began to crane their necks as they snuffled audibly at something they could sense and smell, but could not see.

Link walked a little faster, tightening his grip on

his rifle. He had set this last trap because the place looked like a good coyote crossing, and he either had a catch or else some big animal was very near the trap. The dogs knew the location of every set as well as he did, and always revealed by their actions whether or not there was anything in the next trap. Link brought his rifle halfway up, so he could snap it into shooting position. Coyotes were not dangerous, but if he should have a timber wolf, it would be better to shoot it as soon as possible. Savage and wild when free, wolves were even more so when trapped, and any dog that came within range of their jaws was likely to be killed or at least badly maimed. Good dogs were far too precious to risk near a timber wolf's jaws. Link came around the last bend, to where he could see the jackpine near which he had made the set. He raised his rifle.

The animal in the trap was lying behind the jackpine, peering around the tree, shielding as much of its head and face as possible while it still tried to see. Link looked at the dogs. Ordinarily, when they smelled timber wolves, they were happy to stay as near him as they could get. Now Yuke stood in the trail, hackles raised and lips curled back. The big dog snarled, and his three team mates echoed him. Link looked again at the trap. Was it a wolf, or wasn't it?

Lowering the rifle, with the anxious dogs crowding close at his heels, he walked up the trail until he could see around the jackpine. The animal in the trap tried to run farther around the tree, but the trap chain was already stretched as far as it would go. With no snarl on its face, but defiance and the will to fight plain in its eyes, the beast faced the man and the dogs.

"A dog!" Link cried. "And what a dog!"

He leaned his rifle against a small spruce, took the leashes from his pocket, and chained the pack dogs to four separate trees. Then he walked slowly toward the jackpine and the trapped dog awaiting him there. He ran his eyes admiringly up and down the dog and noted its contours. Then he looked into its eyes, which always offer a fair indication of the intelligence of any dog or man, and whistled.

The dog is an indispensable working companion of the northern trapper, and the speed and distance that trapper can travel depend on the quality of his dogs. Without exception every trapper carries in the hidden reaches of his mind a picture of *the* dog he would like to have, and can never find. But Link was now looking at such a dog.

It looked like an enormous Husky. But it could not be a Husky; its long, trim legs and the bristly whiskers about its mouth were evidences of other breeds. Link stood still, mouth gaping and eyes wide. This dog was the living incarnation of all the great trail mates he had seen in his dreams. Then the truth burst upon him.

"Queen's pup! That's what he is; one of Queen's pups!"

For the big gray dog who, ten months ago, had deserted him to have her puppies in peace, was certainly present in the trapped dog that lay before him. But there was more than that. Link read evidence of the staghound, a mighty breed which, alone and unaided, had coursed and pulled down stags and wolves in the Old World.

Slowly he walked nearer the dog, which lay watching him through intelligent eyes. It did not move, nor flinch, nor betray any of that terror that even some wolves revealed when they were finally trapped. But suddenly it sprang. It came up silently, with no snarl or growl.

Link threw himself backward as the great jaws snapped within inches of his throat, and the dog was brought up short by the trap chain. The man stared at the dog, a puzzled expression in his eyes, then looked at the trail it had made coming here. That trail was not an hour old; the dog could not have been in the trap long enough to have suffered a frozen or broken foot. And the trail came over the ridge, from the direction of the Carney. He stared at the dog again.

"You wouldn't have drifted this far for no reason," he speculated. "Dogs don't wander that far. You met something over there that chased you clean out of the country. Now just what could that be?"

The dog looked at him steadily, and Link set his jaw. Throughout the years he had dreamed of a partner big enough, and strong enough, and sagacious enough, to walk beside him on the lonely trails he had to tread. Here before him he saw the dog of which he had dreamed. It was a wild idea, but any man who did not consider himself at least the equal of any beast had no business on the snow trails. He would tame this dog.

Link went back and opened his pack. He took out a twenty-foot length of the tough rawhide cord he always carried for the hundred and one repair jobs that were always cropping up on the trail. He fashioned a running noose on one end, approached as close to the dog as he dared, and threw his improvised lasso. As it settled over the big dog's head, Link took a half-hitch around a tree. Drawing the knot tight, he cut off the six feet of rawhide that dangled from the end of the thong.

With his belt axe he chopped a two-inch limb

from a spruce and trimmed it until he had a strong stick eighteen inches long. To one end of this he tied the extra length of rawhide. Slipping out of his jacket, he dangled it in one hand, and cautiously walked up beside the trapped beast. Suddenly he threw the jacket.

The big dog caught it in mid-air, dropped it on the snow, and opened his jaws to bite again. Swiftly Link dropped to one knee and thrust his stick between those jaws before they could snap shut. Holding the rawhide thong in one hand, he slid the other across the dog's neck, and around to grasp the other end of the stick. Then he held on desperately. Shackled by the trap and the rawhide noose fastened to the tree, the dog was plunging, digging his claws into the packed snow, struggling to throw his assailant off. Link tried to keep his grasp on the stick, but felt it slipping. He let go with both hands and flung himself sideways.

He rolled over in the snow, and sat up five feet from the dog. The big beast lay still, regarding him intently, but making no effort to stretch the rawhide farther. Link rubbed his throat, and a sensation that was half wonder and half relief rose within him, while he tried to resolve the question in his own mind. As soon as he had known that the dog could get its jaws free, he had thrown himself clear. Even so, he had an uncomfortable impression that he had not acted swiftly enough. Had the dog been able to reach him with those terrible jaws? If so, and he had not slashed when the opportunity was his, it was because he did not want to. It was because he was not a man-killer!

Link rose to his feet, retrieved the stick, ripped the six-foot rawhide thong in two, and tied one end of each half to opposite ends of the stick. He picked up his jacket, which in the scuffle had been thrown clear, and let it dangle from his left hand. Again, carefully, he approached the dog. Again he threw the jacket, extending the stick as he did so.

The dog ignored the jacket, but swung his head to grab the stick and grind it between his jaws. Wildly Link grasped the two ends of rawhide. He ran them behind the dog's ears, looped them so the lacing would not slip, and knotted the thongs together. Stepping back, he wiped the sweat from his face.

"Look, big fella," he said soothingly. "It's just until you and I become acquainted. Honest it is."

The big dog champed his jaws over the stick, trying to spit it out. When he could not he settled back on the snow to look steadily at the man. Link approached again, and gently unfastened the trap. He threw it back against the tree, and set his jaws. It might as well be now as ever. He unfastened that part of the rawhide thong which was knotted around the tree.

Instantly the big dog was away, fighting wildly for the freedom that seemed well within his grasp. Link was jerked violently against the jackpine. Again he took a half-hitch around it, letting the dog fight the thong and wear himself out. Finally, tongue lolling and eyes bulging from the tight noose, the dog settled on the snow to stare at him. Link eased the thong, thus loosening the slip knot, but kept the half-hitch around the tree.

He walked down to the chained dogs, loosened Yuke's pack, and took from it another twenty-foot hank of rawhide. He cut three long lengths, braided them together, and walking slowly up to the captive dog knotted the improvised collar about its neck. Returning to the dogs, he removed the packs from the two biggest and strongest— Yuke and Kena—and led them to the jackpine.

They approached stiff-legged, growling, regarding the wild dog with hostile eyes. Grasping Yuke's collar, Link half dragged him to the side of the wild dog and fastened their collars together with a short length of rawhide. He put Kena on the other side, then grinned at his own handiwork. Somewhere or other he had heard that this was the way captive wild elephants were brought in, and he knew it would take more than his own strength to bring Queen's wild son home to his cabin on the Gander.

Suddenly he thought of Alex Chirikov, the trapper who had come to this wild region and disappeared, just as Queen had done.

"Chiri, that's your name," he told his captive. "Get it?"

He put the discarded dog packs on top of the furs in his own sack and returned to loosen the rawhide thong around the jackpine. Instantly the captive dog was away, bucking and plunging like a horse as he dragged dogs and man with him. Yuke turned, snarling, and his long teeth slashed angrily into the captive's shoulder. Link watched grimly. Yuke could do that now, but when and if this wild hellion ever became broken, or if he was now unfettered, he would kill any dog that dared challenge him.

Inch by inch, aided by the two dogs, Link fought his prisoner away from the jackpine and down to the trail. Tibby and Lud followed wonderingly, for once forgetting rabbits and interested only in the wild dog. Then, when they were within half a mile of the cabin on the Gander, the big masked-face dog began to walk willingly between his two captors. Link watched approvingly. Only the less intelligent creatures fought stubbornly that which could not be successfully battled. Smarter ones yielded, while they awaited that moment when they could do with intelligence what they could not do with strength alone.

Link snubbed the rawhide thong around a tree in front of the cabin, and took a chain from one of the dog houses. With it he tied the captive to the tree. Then he stood still, eyes glowing, and spoke softly to himself.

"Link Stevens, there *can't* be a dog like this one!"

But there was, and he had him. Only one question remained—the question that had arisen at the jackpine, when he had rolled free from the dog, and had not been attacked. Had he just been lucky? He had to know. Resolutely he strode forward and cut the rawhide thongs that bound the stick in the dog's mouth. The stick dropped out. Instantly the dog whipped his head around, and closed his jaws on Link's arm. The man stood perfectly still, neither drawing away nor flinching. The big dog opened his jaws again. There were fang marks on Link's arm, but now he *knew* that this dog was not a man-killer.

Yuke now came forward, bristling. He was the leader of Link's dogs, and meant to maintain that leadership by proving that he was bigger and stronger than any other dog that might enter the pack. Link spoke sharply.

"Yuke!"

The big leader came inquiringly to his side, and when Link slipped the leash back on his collar Yuke sat sullenly down.

"I understand, Yuke," Link said sympathetically. "I know the fight's coming. But let's give him a chance to get acquainted."

He chained the four dogs to their kennels, fed them, and then approached his big captive with a piece of frozen moose meat. The wild dog sat still, his chain slack, and looked steadily at him. Link threw the moose meat down beside him.

"Here you are, Chiri."

The big dog only glanced at the meat, then resumed his steady staring at the man. On sudden impulse Link moved nearer, and when he did the captive dog moved away. Link shook his head.

"You're going to be a tough one, Chiri, but we'll be friends yet."

He went into the cabin, prepared and ate his own supper, then started working on another dog harness. He sewed two heavy canvas bags, and to them attached a rawhide thong to go around the dog's chest, and two lampwick straps to fasten around his belly. All the while he worked he thought of his new dog. Chiri was a problem. Not vicious, but aloof. No killer, but truly wild.

"It'll be a long while before I can trust that one off a leash," Link murmured to himself. "Let him loose and bing! He'll head right back into the woods. But if I can tame him, what a dog he'll be!"

It was almost midnight before he finished the dog pack. He went outside to look at the captive dog, and noted with satisfaction that the chunk of moose meat was no longer there. The dog raised his head. There was a rattling of chains as Yuke, Tibby, Lud, and Kena came out of their kennels to watch. Experimentally Link pulled Chiri's chain. The big dog rose to follow, and Link regarded him quizzically. Independent though Chiri was, he had already learned that it was impossible to fight a chain. But when Link tried to move near so he could stroke his captive's head the big dog moved away again.

"All right, Chiri," Link agreed, "we'll give it up for tonight."

Link went to sleep, but his slumber was broken by troubled dreams of a dog which at first seemed very small because it was far away. As he came nearer, the dog grew in size until he was larger than a horse, and when he opened his jaws they gaped wide enough to engulf a man. Then, just as the dog was about to bite, he dissolved and became a ball of rolling mist that was whisked away by the wind. Suddenly the dog came back, a monstrous thing with glowing eyes that were neither friendly nor hostile, and permitted Link to snap a chain around its neck. Again it disappeared, dissolving into the spruce forest, only to reappear unexpectedly, launching itself from behind a spruce and leaping at him. Link yelled, and woke up sweating.

The first reluctant streaks of the late winter daylight were just beginning to fight their way through the frosted window panes when Link awoke. The outlines of the stoves and cabinets were dim in the feeble dawn. He hurried across the floor to light a fire, but without waiting for the cabin to become warm he dressed and went outside. The troubled dreams of last night remained with him, so that for a moment the capture of Chiri seemed a dream itself. But the dog was still there.

Looking at him, Link suddenly remembered Queen. He had lavished kindness upon the gray dog, but she still hadn't trusted anyone except herself with her puppies. Dogs differed as much as people in their habits, abilities, and personalities. Link stared wistfully at the big masked-face captive. There was a distinct difference between having a dog and owning it. If the dog decided otherwise, then no matter what you did it was never your dog.

As he ate breakfast, Link considered his next

move. The sight of the dog pack he had made last night decided him. Suddenly determined, he carried the pack outside and stood near Chiri. He tried to make his voice soothing, but he could not hide the excitement he felt.

"All right, Chiri, you're going to have your first lesson in packing."

He approached very slowly and carefully, thinking as he did so that he was probably a fool not to have a club in his hand. Only this was a dog he did not want to club; this was a dog he was going to train without one. Link tried to conceal the fear he felt because he knew that a dog could sense fear. Barehanded, he knelt to lay the two canvas sacks, lashed together with rawhide, across Chiri's back. The dog did not move. He fastened the chest strap, tied the lamp-wick binding beneath the dog's belly, and rose to wipe the sweat from his face.

"Whew!" he murmured. "Now I know what it feels like to play with a keg of dynamite—when the fuse is lit!"

He had passed the first hurdle in his training program. The rest was now possible. If this dog had been older, with all the set habits of maturity, there would not be the slightest hope of taming it. But the dog was young and adaptable and because of it might be taught the ways of men. Link looked again at the big dog's proud, intelligent eyes. He could be led, but he couldn't be driven. Link took hold of the chain.

"All right, Chiri. This way."

He smiled with satisfaction when the dog responded. He had learned yesterday's lesson well, and remembered it. For half an hour Link led him back and forth, then left him alone while he did odd jobs about the cabin. The next morning he packed the canvas bags, and again led his pupil about. This time he took him down to the river meadows, so the wild dog and the half-wild pack horses might become acquainted. On the third day he took him out on the trap-line.

They approached a wolf trap that was baited with the same scent that had caught the wild dog, and Chiri sat back to fight the chain. Hastily Link took another half-hitch around a convenient tree, while he smiled to himself. This dog would not be caught twice in the same trap.

He had no trouble with the other dogs. Even though Yuke was obviously jealous of Chiri, he paid little attention to the wild dog while Link was leading him. Still, Link knew that one day Chiri would have to fight Yuke for the leadership of the team, and he also knew what the outcome would be. Yuke was a crafty and vicious fighter who had learned from experts. But the big wild dog was swift as a wolf, and already outweighed Yuke. Hereafter he would keep all five dogs chained at night.

All day and every day they walked the endless trails, and Chiri became stronger and bigger. Link studied him constantly, always looking for a break in the wild reserve, and always disappointed because there was none. When the time came for his mid-year trip to Masland, Link decided to postpone it a week or two more. When he went, Chiri must be ready for civilization.

Meanwhile the mask-face was just another work dog, but a strong and powerful one who was able to pack ten pounds more than even the redoubtable Yuke, and to carry that extra weight over a harder trail. Link was running his lynx and marten sets now; foxes and coyotes had begun to shed their fur soon after the first of the year and were not worth trapping. Mink were still prime, but he had trapped them heavily in the fall, and those that remained were better left as breeding stock. Any trapper who took everything from his own trap-lines cheated himself, because he left nothing for the next year.

The big, shy, ponderous-footed lynx, walking silently as ghosts around their thickets, had better and richer furs than they would have at any other time of the year. With the four other pack dogs in his snowshoe trail, and Chiri constantly on a leash, Link made the rounds of the thickets, reading the stories the lynx had left in the snow. Ranging from kittens to one monster with the biggest track Link had ever seen, they crouched on overhanging logs and stumps near rabbit runs and waited to pounce down on the snowshoes.

Link left his home cabin on a morning so cold that frost seemed to crackle and snap in the very air. His breath vaporized before his nose and mouth, and his nostrils contracted when he breathed. He ducked his nose into his muffler and continued up the trail. Some snow had blown over his usual path, but since he had started packing his trails with the first foot of snow, there was a hard bottom that made for easy walking. The dogs knew as well as he did exactly where the trails were, and they'd stay on them. Sometimes, when the trails were so snowed in that they couldn't be seen, Link could follow them by putting one of the dogs ahead. When a lead dog fell off the trail into soft snow, he simply climbed back onto harder travel.

They came near a thicket wherein there was a lynx set, and the four older dogs began crowding to the outer edges of the trail while they craned their necks and sniffled. On the end of his eight-foot leash, walking just far enough behind so he would not step on the snowshoe trails, Chiri raised his head. Automatically Link's hand went down to his holstered .22. From the dogs' actions, there was something in the trap. He came around a bend to where the side path leading to the trap branched from the trail.

Link tied Chiri to a spruce and walked up the side path. The other four dogs, who had been trained to stay away from trapped animals, lay down on the trail. The trap was set just within a thicket, a wild tangle of windfall, brush, and trash. Link had built a three-foot cubby there, with the bait in the back end and the trap in the narrow entrance. A small lynx was stretched on the snow, spitting and snarling. Link shot it, carried it a hundred and fifty feet away, and pelted it. After resetting the trap, he unfastened Chiri's chain, and went on.

The next two traps held snowshoe rabbits that had been attracted by the smell of the bait inside the cubby, and a whiskeyjack had fallen into the one after that. Link reset the traps, then struck off across a long open meadow that led to another series of thickets. With the five dogs following, he crossed a frozen creek and ascended a little slope that was sparsely dotted with jackpine. Suddenly Chiri growled.

Link stood still, his hand on the grip of his pistol. The other four dogs pricked up their ears and sniffed interestedly, but only the wild dog had been able to detect anything. To the left was a dense thicket, to the right another spacious meadow marked by a series of dips and swales. Chiri snarled, and advanced to the end of his chain, toward the meadow.

Appearing suddenly out of a swale, something sprang into sight. It leaped again, high into the air, making fifteen feet to the jump. Desperately it strove toward the thicket. It was a monster lynx, probably the same one whose tracks Link had seen previously. As he watched, Link saw something else. Straining a hundred yards behind the flying lynx came three gray timber wolves.

Link stood enthralled. He knew that the ancient cat and dog feud prevailed all the way from the back alley of cities to the deepest wilderness, and that coyotes chased lynx whenever they caught them in the open. But this was the first time he had ever seen timber wolves indulging in such sport. Furthermore, they were falling behind. The lynx could run on top of the snow, but the wolves sank through, and had more difficult travel. Flashing into the thicket, the lynx disappeared, the wolves still hot on his trail. Link let the .22 slide back into its holster and grabbed Chiri's chain with both hands.

Lips curled back from long teeth and hackles fiercely bristled, the big dog strained furiously to be free. His claws scraped the packed snow; snow particles flew from beneath his paws. Link snubbed the chain around a tree, and looked knowingly at the wild dog.

"So it's wolves that are bothering you, eh?" he murmured. "It's wolves you don't like."

The big dog flung himself against the chain, and continued to strain toward the thicket. Link hurried forward, with Chiri urging him on, but when he came to that place where the lynx had treed he found only an empty spruce. Hearing or scenting the man and dogs, both wolves and lynx had fled hastily in another direction.

Link grimaced; this was one of the penalties he had to pay for Chiri. Had it not been for the wild dog, he would have been carrying his rifle and thus have been in a position to collect more fur when the lynx and wolves crossed the opening.

They went on, taking such fur as was caught, resetting the traps, and staying overnight in the various out cabins. The ninth day after he had left it, packing some pelts on his own back and the rest on the dogs', Link came back to the cabin on the Gander. He tied and fed the dogs, then hung his green pelts up to cure and put the cured ones in his fur cache. As he fried a moose steak for himself, he looked at the small amount of meat he had left. He'd have to get more, and soon.

The next morning he left the dogs home and went out at daylight with his big .300. He snowshoed up a trapping trail for half a mile, then swung from it to strike across country. The hard crust, with three inches of soft snow on top to act as a cushion, provided ideal snowshoeing. Link went through the spruces to a high knob that overlooked a mass of willows where moose fed. Standing beside a boulder, he waited with his rifle ready.

Far up, a moose appeared in the willows. Link waited, watching the big black beast push down the willow shoots. With maddening slowness it came toward him, eating as it travelled. Link marked an opening about a hundred yards away. When the bull came into that opening, he would shoot. Finally it appeared, but just then a stray breeze blew from Link to the moose.

The bull paused, head up and ears alert, then started to run. Link swung his rifle so the gold-beaded front sight and the notch in the rear sight covered the big shoulder. He fired, and saw the moose go down. It struggled to get up and Link shot again. The moose lay still.

Link snowshoed down, skinned the bull, and quartered it. Carefully he spread the skin on the ground and laid the quarters in it. Then he picked up his rifle and hurried back to the cabin.

At no time was meat left lying out in the open safe meat. In their own season, and when they weren't hibernating, bears found and raided such caches. Coyotes or foxes might get it any time of year, and there were even the swarming snowshoe rabbits, who would turn meat-eaters on occasion.

Link put his rifle in the cabin and lowered his long toboggan from its stand. Ordinarily he would have packed the meat in with the dogs, but the hard crust made for fine toboggan weather and gave him a chance to get all the meat in at once. Link harnessed the dogs, with Yuke in the lead. Then, after some thought, he put Chiri between Yuke and Kena. Both were experienced sled dogs who knew the value of team work, and would punish any sluggard. Standing behind the toboggan, Link cracked his whip over the team.

"Mush!"

The dogs rose, straining into their traces. Chiri got up with the rest and stood uncertainly. Then Yuke pulled him from the front, and Kena nipped his hocks from behind. Chiri moved forward, throwing his weight into the harness, and Link exulted. A dozen times he had thought he could detect something different about the big wild dog: indications that he was winning Chiri over. Now he was sure of it; now he could take his deferred mid-winter trip to Masland. They reached the moose and Link loaded the quarters on the toboggan.

Back at the cabin again, he took the huge liver—a delicacy for men and dogs—and offered half of it to Chiri as a reward. The wild dog looked calmly at him, then moved away and sat down in the snow. Link's face fell. He sighed; the trip to Masland must be postponed again, maybe until summer. Discouraged, he turned back into the cabin.

But if there were any chance of taming that dog, he would gladly postpone a dozen trips to Masland.

9. The Chain

The night wind sighed through the branches of the spruce to which Chiri was chained. Through its steady whisper, the big dog's keen ears were aware of the other dogs changing positions in their kennels, of the soft snaps made by the cooling stove in the cabin, even of the faint creak of the bunk as the man turned over. These were familiar sounds in the pattern of his changing life, to be identified and dismissed as he used to do with the tiny squeaks and murmurs of the forest.

Chiri rose and walked around the tree. Frost lent its sheen to his heavy outer coat, and more frost sparkled in the clear, thin air. When he shook himself, frost flew from him in a misty spray. But no cold penetrated the woven, matted, Husky's coat that lay beneath his outer fur. Chiri was able to face weather that sent the other dogs scurrying to their houses.

He sat down, his bushy tail straight on the snow behind him. Hearing the chain rattle, Yuke came out of his kennel, growling low in his throat. A dim shape in the star-lit night, he stared across the space separating them. Chiri sensed the smoldering resentment that burned within the other dog, and the silent challenge that was hurled across the snow by the big leader of Link's team. Chiri knew that one day he would have to fight Yuke.

He felt no animosity toward the other dog, and was completely undisturbed by thought of the battle to come. He had run in harness with Yuke, knew Yuke's strength and capabilities, and that his own were greater. Meanwhile, he ignored Yuke and the other dogs, satisfied to leave them alone as long as they left him alone.

Turning his back on Yuke, who growled again and crawled back into his kennel, Chiri rose and walked to the end of his chain. He faced east, toward the gorge through which he had run when he raced away from the black wolf and his pack. His front paws did an eager little dance on the snow, and a fierce light such as Link Stevens had never seen burned in his eyes.

A hundred times over he had re-lived the great battle of the windfall, where his mother, brothers, and the one-eyed gray wolf had been killed. A hundred times he had re-lived his escape through the gorge, when the grizzly had unwittingly saved his life. The hate conceived on those two occasions had grown within him day after day. It was a passion that bade him always look toward the Carney, always plot ways of going back there. When he did go back, he would again meet the black wolf, and this time he would not run. In the months Chiri had been with Link Stevens, he had grown. The frightened puppy who had fled through the gorge no longer existed.

And because it was the enemy that kept him from going back through the gorge and finding the black wolf, Chiri also had a great hatred for his chain.

That hatred had begun with the chain on the

wolf trap which had caught him. To Chiri the trap had been an unknown beast, without scent or identification, that had sprung at him out of the snow. He had had half an hour to fight that trap, by every means he knew, before the man had come along, and had not been able to escape because of the chain.

In no way had Chiri connected Link Stevens with the trap, and when Link had taken it from his foot a great respect for a being able to control such a powerful enemy had arisen in the dog's brain. In addition there had been something else, something the dog's ancestry made him sense although he could not understand it. Dogs and men belonged together, and to Chiri Link had been somehow neither entirely strange nor unfriendly. Even when Link had attacked him by thrusting a stick between his jaws, the big dog had instinctively let him go when he might have killed him. He was still puzzled by the things the man called upon him to do, but he obeyed because some inner compulsion told him he must obey. Besides, the man had in no way humbled him nor broken his pride. But the chain did.

As he had done a thousand times before, Chiri began at the nearest link he could reach and, link by link, inspected that chain clear to where it was tied around the spruce. There was no weak spot. As he had done so many times before, the dog took a section of the chain in his mouth and ground his jaws on it. The chain did not yield. He sat down, puzzled and angry. It was impossible to fight a chain; regardless of how it was bitten, clawed, or pulled, it never yielded.

He lay down, facing toward the Carney. He had learned months ago, when crouching beside a rabbit run or stream, awaiting his dinner, that patience was a most valuable asset. He would be patient now. One day, he knew, he would find an opportunity to go back into the wilderness, face the black wolf, and avenge the murder of his mother and brothers. He could wait until that day came.

He slept through the night, but there was still a part of him that never slept. He knew when Yuke came again out of his kennel, but he did not even raise his head. He knew when a soft-footed fox padded near the cabin, and when a winter-lean doe came down to drink at one of the Gander's unfrozen places. He heard the creaking of the bunk as the man got up, and the sound of stockinged feet striking the floor and padding across it. Then came the clatter of stove lids, as wood was thrust into the heating stove. A moment before he could see it, he smelled the wood smoke that arose from the chimney. He heard Link run back across the floor and climb into his bunk to wait until the cabin became warm.

Chiri knew when Link started for the door, but he did not turn his masked face until the man appeared. The wild dog sat still, gazing steadily at Link and awaiting his next move. He offered no greeting, no furiously wagging tail like the other dogs. When Link approached him, Chiri moved away.

A genuine liking had crept into the respect he felt for this man, but to the big dog Link Stevens was very much of an enigma, and he was still too wild to let himself be approached by any creature he could not thoroughly understand. Link was in much the same category as the grizzly; neither had ever offered to hurt him, but might if he was not wary.

Because this was a part of the things he now expected, Chiri stood quietly while Link buckled the pack upon him. Then he waited for Link to release and pack the other four dogs. They crowded forward, a tail-waving procession eager to go on the trail again and resume their everlasting snuffling at rabbit tracks. Chiri himself reflected some of that eagerness; he too liked to be active. But he still held himself aloof.

Several times that day, leading the other dogs, Yuke stopped to look back at Chiri, and throw his silent challenge. The wild dog ignored him. He stayed on the packed trail, just far enough behind Link so that at no time did he step on the tails of the snowshoes. He had learned that to step on them upset both his own balance and that of the man, just as he had learned that to hold back on the chain only tightened the collar about his neck.

That night, again chained to the spruce in front of the home cabin, he stood attentively, watching Link unpack and chain the other dogs and feed them. But only after Link had gone into the cabin, and smoke had begun to curl out of the chimney, did he lie down and start eating his moose meat.

This was once more a normal pattern, but until things were settled in their usual routine Chiri must watch. If anything intruded or threatened, he had to be ready. The cabin window glowed dull yellow when Link lighted his oil lamp and settled down for the evening. Chiri turned again to watch toward the Carney. Months had passed since he was there, but the passage of time had only intensified the memory of the black wolf and his debt to Chiri. The wolf must pay that debt.

When the lamp in the cabin finally went out, the wild dog's eyes glowed again with a savage light, and he turned for another inspection of his chain, link by link, over and over. Baffled once more, he lay down to sleep.

The slow daylight came, and Link carried the five dog packs from the cabin. He dropped four of them in front of the door, fastened Chiri's on, then released the other dogs. They crowded in front of him, tails wagging, eager for whatever this day might bring. Link picked up Kena's pack, tinkered for a moment with a strip of canvas that had started to ravel, and reached for the knife at his belt. The sheath was empty. Link put down the pack and went into the cabin to get the knife.

Soft-footed as a cat, uttering no sound, Yuke stalked toward Chiri as a wolf would stalk another wolf. Tibby, Lud, and Kena squatted on the snow to watch. They would not interfere; this was a fight between their leader and the untried newcomer.

Burdened by the pack, handicapped by the chain, Chiri awaited Yuke's onslaught, only moving a little nearer the tree so there would be more slack in the chain. In so doing, he forgot to keep his head down.

Yuke leaped in, and when his great jaws snapped they closed on the heavy wool that matted Chiri's throat. Only the wild dog's agility saved him. He sidestepped, still careful not to come to the end of his chain. He had learned. From now on, when he fought, he would keep his head down.

Yuke stepped back, his eyes crafty. His first strike had missed, and Chiri's throat was now protected. But the wild dog must have other weaknesses. Yuke advanced slowly, his lips curled but no sound coming from his throat. When he was near enough he feinted at Chiri's shoulder, then swiftly went down to slash at a front leg. But the leg was no longer there.

Chiri's jaws snapped like a wolf trap, and Yuke leaped back, blood dripping from his torn ear. He knew now that, even though packed and chained, the wild dog was a dangerous antagonist. He came on again, leaping in with all the strength in his powerful body, then swerving to bump Chiri's shoulder with his own. Yuke intended to throw the other dog down, and leap on him when he rolled in the snow.

But the masked-face dog met his charge squarely. When Yuke would have wheeled, Chiri struck. His great jaws closed on Yuke's neck and gripped tightly. Yuke's breath became a rattle; he scraped frantically with his claws. But slowly, inexorably, he was lifted into the air. Chiri's jaws ground deeper; the wild dog tasted blood.

"Chiri! Yuke!"

Chiri dropped his enemy and backed to the end of his chain. He stood there calmly watching Link. The man stared at him, and at the chastened Yuke. He shook his head wonderingly. He had known that Chiri possessed enormous strength, but it was incredible that any dog should possess enough power in his jaws alone to lift the ninety-pound Yuke into the air.

Tibby, Lud, and Kena had also formed their opinion of the fight. They still respected Yuke, but their fear of him was gone. The pack had a new leader.

10. Trouble on the Gander

The spring break-up was late. By the middle of March, near the time when the ice usually split and piled up in the Gander in big blocks, the temperature dropped suddenly to forty below zero, as the waning winter fought savagely to retain its hold on the wilderness. On the wide Gander meadows, Link's three pack horses huddled behind whatever offered shelter, and looked inquisitively toward the cabin. They had nothing to mark the passage of time except an instinct which told them that, though it was still cold winter, the summer would soon be here and they would have to go to work again.

The horses were not the only creatures which foresaw the imminent approach of spring. High in the air, the pair of long-necked, white-throated geese who were sure of finding open water when they returned to their usual nesting grounds, beat against the cold as they flew laboriously northward. Gabbling querulously, the geese circled their pond and finally came to rest not on open water, but on the unyielding ice. That night, when the geese had bent their heads under their wings to keep their eyes from freezing, a prowling coyote pounced on them. In dying, the two wanderers' feebly beating wings seemed to drum a requiem to their fruitless, hard flight.

Link Stevens, too, knew that spring would come, but so far he felt only the cold and saw the pitiless winter. He tallied up the small fortune that lay in his fur cache, and bit the end of his pencil thoughtfully. It had been a good season. Fur trapping was always a gamble, but this year he had won.

Link sat back in his chair and thought of Masland. There were cities beyond that little frontier town, a whole world outside the wilderness, and he had furs enough to afford some of its luxuries. Although at the moment he felt that he would never return to the Gander once he was out of it, he knew that he would return; he was a trapper because only as a trapper could he live as he wished. The wild places were part of him.

But right now he was lonely. To break the mood, Link went out to look at Chiri. The big dog, thinking the thoughts which he was willing to share with no one else, lay under the spruce to which he was always chained when they were at the home cabin. Link felt a great frustration. He had to have this dog, and some day Chiri would have to have him. When that day came Link knew that he would never again be lonely. But the day seemed a long way off.

Meanwhile there were muskrat traps to set and tend. As soon as the ice broke from any creek or pond Link shoved his log raft out to make his sets. After he had caught all the muskrats he thought should be taken at that spot, he pried the spikes out of the raft, and went on to make another raft on some other pond, creek, or river.

Then came the day when a long V line of honking geese appeared in the sky, and two by two the migrants dropped out of formation to descend to favorite nesting places. Ducks flew eyerywhere, and flowers bloomed at the very edges of those stubborn snow drifts which, lying in the shade of spruces or thickets, refused to melt. The sun rose earlier and stayed later, and everything that had ever wanted a nest or home seemed to be seeking it. After a dead winter, when the wilderness seemed inhabited exclusively by deadly or fear-filled things, it had again come alive. Link pulled all his traps, and the next morning went down to the meadows to catch his pack horses.

The three horses looked at him, then kicked up their heels and, with manes and tails flying, galloped up the now lush river flats. With a rope coiled in his hand Link followed patiently, and finally cornered one of the chestnuts against a windfall that the horse could not break through. Link threw a loop around the horse's neck, and hand over hand drew himself to the squealing, fighting horse. Patting the half-wild thing on its trembling nose, he looped the rope around the horse's muzzle, took a half-hitch to form a crude hackamore, and made a flying mount. He let the horse buck and plunge until it had worked off its excess spirits. With one horse already captured it was easy to catch the other two.

Thirteen days later, with all five dogs on leash and the tired pack horses walking ahead, Link came into Masland and Pete Roberts' store. The old storekeeper ambled lazily out on the porch.

"Well, well! If the wild man ain't back! How'd it go, Link?"

"All right."

Pete's eyes rested on Chiri. He gave a low whistle of admiration.

"Where'd you get a dog like that?"

"Caught him in one of my wolf traps. I'm sure he's one of the pups of that gray bitch, Queen, that ran away last year."

"Well, I'll be switched! Want to sell him?"

"Nope."

"I'll give you five hundred."

Link laughed, and Pete's keen old eyes rested for a moment on the younger man's face. He, too, knew the snow trails and the wilderness, and what an exceptional dog could mean to a man. This was such a dog, and Link knew it.

"Well, bring your catch in, Link. I reckon you're willing to sell that."

"It's a good one, Pete, and it'll take a lot of money to buy it."

"I think I can scrape up enough," the storekeeper chuckled. "How long you stayin' this time?"

"I don't know."

"It won't be more'n three days," Pete grunted positively. He picked up one of the pack boxes and carried it inside. As they unpacked and sorted the furs, they exchanged bits of news. Pete finished his tally sheet, and shoved that and a roll of bills across to Link.

"I've took out for your grubstake, here's some for fun, and here's what you got left. Have yourself a time. Your grubstake will be ready in three days."

"Suppose I don't go back in three days?"

"You will, but make sure you tie that big dog so's nobody can't steal him."

"I wouldn't want to be the one who tried it," Link retorted, dryly.

Link was glad to be heading back toward the

Gander. As he turned the dogs loose beyond the last house, he chuckled. For once he had been right and old Pete Roberts wrong. He had stayed five days in Masland, two more than he had ever stayed before, and Pete had loudly proclaimed himself betrayed. Link had stayed the extra time because he had hoped so doing would help break Chiri.

He glanced down in perplexity at the big dog padding beside him. For four days he had spent all his time hunting up every trapper in town, and taken them to old Pete's barn to see Chiri. All of them had been excited about the dog, and most had wanted to buy him, but the big mask-face had merely looked at them with his strange wild eyes and remained in the shell he had built around himself. The sight of other people, and the fact that none had offered him harm, had meant nothing to him. He was as aloof as ever. For a moment Link felt a wild impulse to cut Chiri's collar and give him that freedom for which he was so obviously yearning. Then he shut his mind to the thought. There were thousands of dogs on the snow trails, but only one like this. He would win him over yet.

The pack horses trotted ahead, snatching at grass whenever they thought they were safely out of Link's reach, then trotting on again as he came up. Yuke, Tibby, Lud, and Kena cast frantically about on their everlasting business of sniffling at rabbits, but every now and again one of the four looked back at Chiri. Link saw them, and knew why they were doing it. Chiri had proven himself better than Yuke, and was their rightful leader, but because of a man's will Yuke continued to lead the pack. Link clamped his jaws grimly.

In a sense both pack horses and ordinary pack dogs were only the labor to do what a trapper could not do for himself. But a good lead dog was the trapper's right arm, and as such beyond price. Maintaining discipline among the rest of the pack was only part of a leader's job. He must know all the trails, and know them so well that, even if his master was suddenly stricken blind, the lead dog could and would guide him over those trails. He must at all times know how to get himself, his pack mates, and his master, out of trouble should they get into it. And he must be absolutely dependable. That was the kind of dog Link wanted, and had never had. He looked down at Chiri.

"All the things you could be—and the things you are," he said aloud. "Chiri, why don't you unbend?"

They arrived at the Cumber, and after he had set his camp up Link went down to catch grayling for the dogs and himself. He caught nothing on his first cast, nor his second, nor his third. A puzzled look flickered across his eyes. The Cumber had always yielded grayling and seldom had he needed more than a half-hour to catch the first one; but it was two hours before he had even a meager meal for the dogs and himself. That in itself was unimportant; the dogs were accustomed to missing an occasional meal and he could always tighten his belt. Probably, for some unknown reason, the grayling were just not hitting flies today.

It was not until he had gone three days farther along the trail that Link knew definitely that this was going to be one of the lean years that occasionally struck the wilderness. The snorting deer that formerly jerked their heads in alarm and bounded out of his way every half-mile or so were now much harder to find, and once he traveled half a day without seeing any. Every thicket, or so it seemed, used to hold a surly bull moose or a ner-

vous cow, anxious about her gangling calf. Now he
saw no moose. Questing eagerly for fresh rabbit
tracks, the dogs found few. Even the friendly
spruce hens and ptarmigan were not nearly so
plentiful.

Link kept on. He who selected a trapper's life
made a hard contract between nature and himself,
one that included taking the bad as well as the
good. The one who would meet a bad year, and
still go on, more than earned the right to whatever
the next good year might bring with it.

They came to the Carney, and started up the
grassy meadows toward Two-Bird Cabin. Just as
they came in sight of the cabin, Chiri growled. A
second or two later the other four dogs bristled.
With an instinct born of long practice, and a full
realization of what it meant when trail dogs
growled, Link stepped back to grasp the horses'
halter ropes, which had been left looped over the
pack saddles. The roan horse snorted nervously.

He led the horses to one of the small trees that
grew in the Carney meadows and tethered them.
There was certainly something up ahead, and he
didn't want the horses to stampede. Link slipped
his rifle out of its scabbard on top of one of the
horse's packs and, holding Chiri's chain, advanced
cautiously.

With every evidence of fear, the other four dogs
came in to slink behind him. Alert and unafraid,
Chiri walked beside him. Link came nearer the
cabin, and heard the unmistakable sound of an
angry bear snapping its jaws.

Link dropped Chiri's chain, stepping on it while
he gripped the rifle with both hands. He always
kept a small stock of food at Two-Bird, and no
doubt a passing black bear had smelled that food
and was trying to get it. Raiding bears that broke

into cabins were nothing new or unusual, and he could take care of this one. Furthermore, he needed a bear. Bear fat, properly rendered, was as good as lard for cooking and better than oil for greasing leather shoes and harness. Link cocked the rifle.

Like a miniature tornado, a medium-sized grizzly burst around the corner of the cabin. Mouth open, bristling, it charged straight at him.

Link shot coolly and methodically, trying to place his bullets in that gaping red mouth or in the bear's chest. Beside him Chiri, who since infancy had known grizzly bears, sat quietly and awaited developments. The other dogs crowded close at his heels. The bear staggered, ran a few more steps, and collapsed in a motionless heap.

Curiously Link inspected it, and the cold little foreboding that had come to his mind back on the Cumber seemed to have a stronger grip. Few bears wantonly attacked human beings. If this one had located a food cache, and was so desperately hungry that it would defend that cache even against a man . . . . Link put the thought from his mind and skinned the bear.

For two days he lay over at the cabin, trying out the bear's fat and cutting wood to swell the depleted supply. Then they went on.

When they came to the Gander, Link looked across the river to see two velvet-horned bucks browsing in the meadow within twenty feet of the cabin. He shot one in its tracks, and smiled to himself. He had chosen the Gander primarily because it was a wild, free, and unspoiled country that appealed to him. Secondly, the Gander had plenty of wild life and a man would never go hungry there. Now he had proven it by finding game right on his doorstep. Probably it was only in that section between the Gander and Masland that game had struck its low cycle.

But when he went out on the trap-lines Link knew that the Gander, too, hadn't nearly as much game. Where there had been signs of ten foxes or coyotes last year, there was one this year. Big game was scarce and the almost limitless snowshoe rabbits had dwindled away noticeably.

Link faced the situation for what it was. All game had its high and its low cycles. Last year had been high, and for some unaccountable reason this year was low. But trapping was not simply a matter of buying traps and setting them. A successful trapper, in addition to knowing everything he could about the habits of fur animals, had to know the country he trapped just as thoroughly. He might not make expenses on the Gander this year, but he would learn something. Grimly he settled down to the double task of finding food and running his depleted trap-lines.

Then, one overcast day, a dusting of snow drifted out of the sky. Chained to their kennels, the hungry dogs licked their chops and whined as the snow brought memories of feasts they had eaten on winter hunts. Link went down to the Gander, casting from the bank with a heavy hook and using some of his precious venison for bait. He caught trout, but not nearly as many as he should. He shared his food with the dogs. If their bellies became lean, so did his.

He had to have meat, he knew that. Day after day, giving up time that should have been spent improving his trap-lines, he walked the muskeg and the ridges looking for game. Once he shot a small buck, and the next day, a half-grown caribou. Carefully he hung them up to freeze, while he worked the trap-lines and hoped to get more food.

Little by little he parcelled out the frozen meat and the precious food he had brought from Masland to himself and the dogs.

Now he lived on hope that, when the year advanced, the game would come back. If it did, if he was able to get enough food, he still might have a good year when lynx and marten trapping came into its own. But the game did not come back, and his food supplies dwindled day by day.

One cold morning he packed the dogs to go out on the trap line. With Chiri chained, as usual, and the other four running behind, he struck out toward Goose Creek cabin.

He was on top of a ridge when he saw the thing move. It was in the valley below him, among some small evergreens. Link stood still, holding his breath and praying the dogs would create no disturbance to frighten whatever might be near. Then he saw its outline.

It was a moose, a huge bull with a mighty bell and great, polished antlers. Like a ghost it was moving away from him, fading silently into the spruces. The bull had either heard or scented him and the dogs. Link breathed a silent prayer as he raised his rifle; a big bull like this would furnish meat for a long time to come. But almost before the blast of his rifle had lost itself in echoes he knew that he had missed.

The dogs knew that the sound of a gun meant game, and now they stood eagerly, watching the place from which the scent of the bull drifted back to them. Link quickly stripped their packs off, chivvying the dogs on as he did so.

"Hi! Hi! Take 'em!"

The four dogs rushed pell-mell down the ridge. Yelling and barking, they dashed into the spruces. Link stared long and searchingly at Chiri. Then, suddenly, he whipped out his knife and cut the rawhide collar. Some time he had to trust the big dog, and that time was now. This was an emergency; if he did not somehow manage to get food for both himself and the dogs, then they could not possibly stay here longer. But the four, Link knew, would run the moose only a little way. If Chiri was with them, they might run far enough to bay their game.

Without a backward glance, the big dog bounded swiftly down the slope. Rifle dangling from his right hand, Link ran after him.

He found the bull's track, with the tracks of the five dogs upon it, and followed as fast as he could. An hour later, panting, tired, he met four dogs coming back, led by Yuke. Chiri was not with them. Link ran on down the track and found where the four had left it to return. Chiri alone had gone on. Blindly, heedless of the whipping branches that slapped across his face, Link continued on the track of the moose and dog. Only with darkness did he leave it, his heart sinking. He had built up so many plans around the big wild dog, so many hopes that, when the right time came, Chiri would not fail him.

But Chiri *had* failed him. He had gone back to the wilderness.

Link returned to the cabin on the Gander, and sat moodily staring at the frosted window, listening to the rising wind. Then his jaw tightened. He still had the three horses. He would kill one and stay on the Gander anyway. But for the first time since he could remember, he was afraid.

Early the next morning, rifle in hand, he went down to the river flats where the horses grazed. He stood in unbelief, looking at the vast number of tracks that had never been imprinted by horses' hooves. Emboldened by their hunger, more afraid of starvation than they were of attacking beasts that belonged to man, a pack of wolves had come while he was away. There was nothing left of the horses save a few cracked bones to which not a shred of flesh clung.

Link strode wearily back to the cabin. There was nothing he could do now save admit defeat and go back to Masland.

11. The Bull Moose

The big bull moose was one of the few creatures
on the Gander whose belly had not been pinched
by hunger. He was not a meat-eater, and could still
ride the willows down with his chest and eat the
tender shoots. Ugly and solitary, the bull had
never joined the fall herds when they had congre-
gated after the battles of the mating season. When
the rest of the moose migrated, he had simply
remained on the Gander. And now that most of the
others were gone, the bull could select for himself
the best and tenderest food.

He was on his way to feed on a patch of willows
that grew along the Gander when he smelled Link
Stevens and the dogs. Instantly the bull stopped.

He knew Link because he had often crossed the
man's snowshoe trails and paths, and the scent was
familiar. But the bull was not an untried yearling
who would break and run at the first alarming
noise; he was a mature old beast who had become
old because he acquired wisdom when he was
young.

He had a great respect for the rifle Link carried;
four times in four years the bull had stood near
other moose and heard the smash of that rifle. He

had seen other moose go down, so he understood the force of that rifle. And twice in four years the bull had been stalked by Link. Both times he had escaped by stealth. The bull was perfectly aware that Link could not harm him unless he could see him.

Just outside the curtain of spruces, the bull remained perfectly still while he tested the wind currents with his nose and flipped his ears back and forth the better to hear. A split second before Link saw him, the wind brought the man's exact location to the bull's nose. Silently, careful to make no noise that would betray him, the bull faded into the spruces. He heard the rifle's smash, and began to run. Once again he intended to make good his escape.

The bull accepted pursuit as a probability rather than a possibility, and even before he was certain pursuit would follow, he laid plans to circumvent it. He was not greatly worried, because he was in the shelter of the spruces. Nevertheless, if he wished to remain out of danger, he must overlook nothing.

He had been running on a good moose trail because it offered the most convenient method of flight. Now he slowed to a walk, took a faint trail that led through the spruces, found another moose trail, and travelled back in the direction from which he had come. He was aware of the peril lying in that direction, but the bull wanted to know exactly where the man and dogs were. A minute later, with the wind again blowing directly into his nostrils, the bull smelled the four dogs sweeping along behind him.

He was not greatly disturbed. He had fought off timber wolves several times, and once had even been overtaken by Link Stevens' four dogs on one

of their nocturnal hunts. They had set upon him
with growls and snarls, but a few sweeps of his
antlers and a few strikes with his mighty front
hooves had sent them on their way. They were not
dangerous.

Still, he began to run again, partly because of the
dogs and partly because, somewhere back of those
dogs, the man might be coming along, and if the
bull did not greatly fear the dogs he was afraid of
the man. Silently, but still keeping the wind blowing from the dogs to himself, the bull raced along
one of the many moose paths that threaded the
spruce forest. Now, in addition to smelling the
dogs, he could hear them in full cry.

Stopping, the bull swung half around with his
head high and his sloping rear quarters against a
spruce. For a few seconds, reading the wind with
his nose and flipping his ears alternately back and
forth to catch any sound, he stood still. When he
ran on he did not travel quite so swiftly. He had
heard the dogs and scented them, but so far there
was nothing else on his trail. The bull knew what
he could do with the dogs, and that it would take
no more than a few moments to discourage or kill
them. There was no need to run very fast.

Just ahead there was a small opening, set like a
patch of foam in a great sea of forest. The wind had
swept the snow across this clearing, piling it in a
high drift that dropped away in an almost vertical
wall of snow. In front of that drift, knowing that the
dogs could not get at him from the rear, the bull
turned to defend himself. He pawed the snow and
reached down to scrape the ground with the tip of
one great palmated antler. He angrily stamped his
front feet, packing the snow in front of him. Neck
bristling, eyes gleaming redly, the bull awaited
the coming of the dogs.

He could hear them now, scarcely two hundred yards away and still sweeping along in full cry. The bull backed a little nearer the drift and once more raked the snow with his antlers. Then the dogs came.

With Yuke in the lead, straining fifteen yards ahead of Kena, they swept out of the spruces and stopped. The bull grunted, and alternately lifted both great, split front hooves. Yelling hysterically, Tibby ran to one side and swerved. Yuke came next, bristling and snarling.

With a little bound the embattled bull left his protecting drift and charged forward. At once he had sensed his advantage. These were work dogs, not hunters, and even Yuke hadn't the slightest idea of how to go about pulling down a bull moose that showed fight. Tibby ran first, then Lud. Somewhat reluctantly, Yuke and Kena followed, dodging into the spruces when the bull charged them. They were hungry, but not hungry enough to fight anything so huge and ferocious. Their master had always fed them, and he would again. Anything they had ever killed hunting had been only an extra tidbit, something that could be added to their regular meal, and they preferred rabbits.

At the edge of the clearing the bull stopped, satisfied to let his fleeing enemies run. He stamped his heavy hooves again, ready to renew the battle should the dogs decide to do so, and raised his head to sniff the breeze. The scent of the dogs faded, and slowly the bull's bristled mane relaxed.

At a slow walk now, the bull went on down the snow-covered moose path. Two grouse, eating buds from a birch that had stolen a place in the spruces, thundered away on beating wings and dived into a friendly spruce. One of the few red squirrels still left in the Gander darted to the top of a tree, and silently watched the bull pass.

The bull trotted a little way, sure of his own power. All seemed serene in this depth of forest. The bull pawed in the snow, nosing at the lichens and frozen bushes but hungry for tender willows. He wandered off the moose path through some sparse-growing spruces, looking for a sheltered place where he might rest until night made it safe to go out to a willow patch.

Suddenly he tensed himself, tossing his head and testing the wind that eddied around his nostrils; another dog was coming. It was not one of those which had been with the four, but certainly it had been with the man. The bull shook his antlers angrily, and began to run once more. But he did not run very far. When he came to a windfall he swung with his back against it, his antlers ready to impale and his heavy hooves to strike anything that came near. The moose ran a little way from the windfall and back to it, trampling the snow so it would not hinder his movements when he had to move swiftly. Then, with his rump brushing the windfall, he stood ready to meet the dog.

The dog came on, mouth open and tongue lolling. The bull grunted warningly, and reached down to scrape the snow with his antlers. But the moose did not rush out in a savage charge. The four dogs he had recognized as puny enemies, and had not hesitated to attack them. This dog was as big as the largest wolf the moose had ever seen; the bull's wild-given knack of judging his enemies made him recognize in Chiri a formidable opponent. The bull knew that, even though he was faced by only one dog instead of four, he must make no mistakes.

The dog swerved to the left, and the big bull

whirled to defend himself from that side. Chiri ran to the right, again to be confronted with broad and impregnable antlers that were both weapons and armor, and by the heavy war maces that were the bull's smashing front hooves. There was death in every delicate tracing on those antlers, and in every smooth curve of each polished hoof. The bull stood breathing defiance through his nostrils. He knew he was safe here, and that he could kill the thing menacing him should that thing dare attack.

When the dog lay full length in the snow, the bull backed once more against the windfall so he could protect his rear and flanks. The moose, too, had learned the value of patience, and was prepared to maintain his defensive position for as long as might be necessary. He stamped his front hooves, a little uneasy because the dog was lying so quietly instead of rushing in as the other dogs had done.

All that night, while the wind blew ceaselessly, driving more snow ahead of it, the embattled moose stood with his back against the windfall while the watchful dog studied his every move. The rays of a half moon filtered dimly through the storm, giving just enough light for the moose to see the dark shape of the dog lying on the snow. The bull shuffled his hooves uneasily and tossed his head. His great stomach was beginning to rumble in protest because it was empty. But it was far better to remain hungry than to venture out where the enemy awaiting him could slash at his unprotected belly and flanks. The bull tossed his great antlers again, and his red eyes reflected the anger he felt because he did not dare venture out to battle a thing not one-fifth his size. But he was no fool.

A slow, reluctant dawn filtered out of the sky to spread itself over the snow-covered wilderness. The bull raised his head, shaking away the snow that had plastered itself against the broad palms of his antlers, and looked with raging eyes at the silent dog. If he could only get at that thing he knew that he could kill it with one blow of a hoof or one strike of his antlers. But the bull also knew that if he charged, the dog would dance before him, and leap in to strike his hock or belly. He had to stay where he was, protected by the windfall; it was more important to be alive than it was to eat.

Then, toward the middle of the day, the moose looked and the dog was gone. A moment before it had been there, and its scent still remained heavy in the air, but the bull was unable to see or hear his enemy. Too knowing to rush into anything that merely looked safe, the moose waited. But as he did so he formed a plan.

This was his country, the place in which he had been born, and he knew every hump in the muskeg, almost every tree in the forest. Less than a hundred yards away was another windfall where he could find protection for his back and sides, should the dog's absence prove to be a trick. The bull cautiously moved ten feet from the windfall and stood still. When half an hour passed and nothing happened, he started to run. He pounded the hundred yards to the next windfall and backed against that. For a long while he stood, testing the air currents with his nose and flicking his ears back and forth while he listened. He could still smell the dog, but it had lain a long while before him and its scent would remain.

As the bull considered his next move, he thought of the willows and the tender shoots that his belly craved. There was a big willow patch only a half-mile away, and between it and this windfall was a great gray boulder from which he could fight if he had to. The moose dashed out from his defensive position and started to run. Like a huge gray arrow, the dog was upon him, flashing from the spruces where a second ago there had been nothing.

As it came it struck at the bull's hock. The big dog slashed as it leaped, and the bull felt the strong tendon that controlled his right hind leg slip like a taut, suddenly released string. When the moose whirled to strike, the dog danced out of his way. Again the moose turned to run, but he could not control his right hind leg.

He struck clumsily as the dog came in again, leaping at the bull's soft, unprotected under belly. A great stream of blood gushed down on the snow. The bull was swinging crazily now, striking at shadows with his hooves and antlers. For a moment he felt sharp pain as the tendon in his other hind leg was severed, then his eyes began to glaze. He was scarcely aware when the dog leaped at his throat.

Chiri stood over his kill, a wild dog who had succeeded where a man had failed.

12. The Trail to Masland

Link Stevens fed his four dogs well that night, then loaded four packs with camping and trail equipment and such food as remained. He threw Chiri's pack into a cupboard and did not look at it again. He had been a fool to build his hopes around taming a wild dog, or thinking of Chiri and himself as an invincible team. Old Pete Roberts would sure have a good laugh when he saw him coming back from the Gander, with his tail between his legs like any whipped puppy.

At the same time he was aware that it was not Pete Roberts' opinion that bothered him, nor even his own failure to tame the wild dog. It was something far more important, something he did not like to admit even to himself. He was running away. He had never been afraid of the wilderness before, but since it had whipped him, he knew that from now on he would always be afraid of it.

Bitterly he moved about the cabin, preparing a supper for which he had no appetite. Then he kicked his pacs off and sought the familiar comfort of his bunk. But he could not sleep; a great restlessness kept prodding him. He had fought as hard as he could against taking the trail to Masland, but now that he had admitted defeat, it seemed that he should start at once. Anything was better than staying here. Long before it was light enough to travel he got out of his bunk to start a fire and cook breakfast. He was not hungry, but forced himself to eat. A man hitting a long trail had to eat, and there was enough food to last through to Masland. He would not have to stint either himself or the dogs.

Link washed the dishes, swept the cabin, and packed the dogs. They stood in front of the cabin, tails wagging and eager as they waited for their master to come out and show them the trail they would take this day. Link shoved the .22 pistol into its holster, took his big rifle in the crook of his arm, closed the cabin door behind him, and hit the trail to Masland.

Always before he had stopped to look back at the cabin, but this time he did not. There was a finality about this departure that had never been present before. He started out with long strides; he wanted desperately to talk to someone, and the sooner he reached Masland the sooner he would know relief from the loneliness and fear that had attacked him.

They came to the bank of the Gander, and Link glanced up and down the long river. Except for open channels where the water flowed very swiftly, it was frozen solid. The wind had swept most of the snow from the ice, and it lay clear and shining, like a great, long ribbon of glass. Link unlaced his snowshoe harnesses—snowshoes slip badly on ice—and with them in his left hand started across the river. Gingerly, trying their best to maintain a balance on the smooth ice, the dogs strung out behind him.

Link was halfway across when, without any warning, he slipped and went down. He struck hard, but the pack on his shoulders cushioned the fall and he twisted to take the rest on his hips. The rifle flew out of his hand, and slid like a long skate across the smooth ice. The four dogs stared curiously at their suddenly prostrate master.

Link put both hands on the ice and pushed himself to a sitting position. He rose painfully, rubbing his hip. He walked over to pick up the rifle, anxiously examined the sights, and lifted it to shooting position. Sighting on a small ice hummock a hundred yards up the river, he squeezed the trigger. The big gun roared, and the ice hummock disappeared in a shower of ice dust and splinters. Link heaved a sigh of relief, then knelt to look at his snowshoes. They were unbroken. He had been lucky; a trapper's rifle and snowshoes are his most valuable possessions. Cautiously, making sure that he did not fall again, Link continued across the river and up the trail on the other side.

Three miles farther on he stopped to rest himself and the dogs; despite his snowshoe trail they were making heavy going in the two and a half feet of new snow that had fallen. Just ahead, passing between a stump and a spruce, were broad tracks recently left by a passing snowshoe rabbit. Link glanced quizzically at the dogs. They must have smelled the trail and known perfectly well that the rabbit had passed. They should be interested. Instead, the four seemed to have no desire other than staying as near him as they could get. Link looked around nervously.

Never before had he seen the wilderness exactly like this. Its silence was unbroken even by the jeering chuckle of a whiskeyjack. Link stared intently at the rabbit track; in a wilderness where only the marks of a passing rabbit broke an endless blanket of snow, everything seemed utterly dead. Link thought of the many and varied tracks he would ordinarily see, and again felt a thrill of fear and strangeness.

Defiantly he shook off the feeling; the dogs were not staying near because they too sensed something dire and dismal, but because they were tired from walking in the deep snow. Link continued down the trail, speculating about the plans he had made before leaving the Gander.

Two-Bird Cabin was fifty miles out, and he had wanted, by forced travelling, to get there by noon of the second day. Then they could rest half a day before going on. But in this travelling, unless there was less snow farther down the trail, he would not reach Two-Bird before evening of the second day. Well, he could do without any rest. Travel would be easier as he got near Masland. Somebody was always using the trails near town and almost certainly they would be broken out.

Yuke whined anxiously, and Link stopped to turn around and look at the big dog. Yuke was travelling so near his heels that his nose was almost bumping the snowshoe tails, and Tibby, Lud, and Kena were crowding as close behind as they could get. Link stared at Yuke, puzzled. An experienced trail dog who knew every phase of wilderness life, it was not like him to take meaningless alarm or give a false warning. Link spoke gently.

"What's the matter, Yuke?"

The big lead dog whined again, and looked back into the impenetrable spruces. Then he advanced to Link's feet and crouched, shivering. Obviously afraid of something which they too could sense, the other three dogs crowded up until they were touching each other.

Link shifted the rifle so he could grasp it with both hands and be ready to shoot at a second's notice. Again he felt a cold little tremor along his spine, and thought he understood.

When hairy men lived in caves, and existed entirely by hunting, they too could read the scents carried on the wind and hear the tiniest rustle. As they discovered new and easier ways to get game, and finally were able to live without hunting at all, those senses atrophied until even the dullest animal was keener than the keenest man. But wilderness men still retained a vestige of those senses, a sort of sixth sense that warned them of things they could neither see nor hear. Without being able to identify whatever troubled the dogs, Link still knew that peril was afoot.

Probably it was a hungry grizzly. When they were well fed and fat, grizzlies hibernated as soon as the weather became cold enough. But in a lean year like this, when their flanks were not padded with the fat upon which they must exist all winter, they did not hibernate until they were forced to, and some grizzlies remained abroad all winter. Link had faced charging grizzlies before, and though they were not pleasant things to meet, he could take care of one if he had to. He spoke reassuringly to the dogs.

"It's all right. Everything's all right."

He went on, travelling carefully and always watching the places where trees grew right down to the trail. A hunger-mad grizzly was very cunning and perfectly capable of planning an ambush. They came to a long stretch of trail that was flanked on both sides by heavy spruces, and Link watched Yuke closely as he made his way through it. He breathed in relief as soon as they were on the other side, where the spruces receded and a series of little meadows flanked the trail. Crowding as close as they dared to his snowshoes, the dogs kept looking anxiously back over their shoulders. Link was brought up a second time by a snarl and a short, choppy bark from Yuke.

He swung around, quickly this time, because he sensed that whatever was trailing them had come very near. With ruffs bristling and lips curled back in snarls, the dogs pushed up until they were ringed all about him. All four were gazing to the right and back along the trail. Link stared in amazement.

A hundred and fifty yards back, and to the right of the trail, a great, gray timber wolf had come out of the spruces. It was an ugly thing with a scarred face and tattered ears. Slatted ribs stood out like steel bars; its paunch was so gaunt that the wolf seemed to have no belly, but only hips, back, and chest. It sat in the snow in plain sight, staring hard at the man and the dogs.

Link couldn't believe his eyes. During four years in a wilderness in which timber wolves abounded, he had never been able to get within rifle range of one. Despite their reputed ferocity, they feared men mightily, and were so keen of scent that they always knew when a man was around. Under ordinary circumstances, nothing was shyer than a timber wolf. Link closed his eyes momentarily, but when he opened them again the wolf was still there. Once more Link felt that cold shiver run up and down his spine. No trapper feared normal timber wolves, but Link had often speculated as to what a pack might do if it became hungry enough. Here was *one* wolf hungry enough to overcome his fear of man!

Slowly Link raised his rifle, brought the front and rear sights to bear on the gray wolf's chest, and squeezed the trigger. A hollow click snapped mockingly in the cold air. As though it were grinning at him, the gray wolf opened its mouth and ran its tongue out. Link lowered the rifle, pumped a fresh shell into the chamber, sighted, and pulled the trigger again. There was another futile click as the bolt descended on the firing pin. Feverishly Link injected another cartridge, and another, and another. The five cartridges that had been in his rifle, five deadly things capable of killing moose and grizzlies, became five tiny marks in the snow as he pumped them out. Link drew the bolt to inspect the mechanism, and his face turned white.

The firing pin was gone. No doubt it had broken when the rifle skidded on the ice, and the pin had remained in the bolt only long enough to fire the test cartridge. The recoil of that had knocked the pin out, and left him with a rifle that would not shoot. Link drew the tiny, ineffective pistol from its holster, rested the barrel across his wrist, aimed high so the little pellet would carry, and squeezed the trigger. The .22 snapped like a breaking twig.

The wolf in the clearing rose indolently and walked back into the sheltering spruces. Link stood still, feeling the cold sweat on his forehead and sensing the fear in the dogs. At this season wolves usually travelled in packs, and if there was one on his trail its pack mates could not be far away. Link looked again at his broken rifle, and stared down the trail.

It was very narrow just ahead, with thick, stubby spruces coming almost to the trail's edge and growing in wild profusion to form an unbreakable wall of green. A mile and a half beyond the narrow part was a wide opening flanked by dead trees. Link glanced at the sky. It was only about two o'clock and he had plenty of time before darkness set in. He'd better go to that clearing, gather a great quantity of wood for a fire, and prepare to defend himself should the pack attack at night. It was unheard of that wolves come near a fire, but it was also unheard of that one wolf should sit and watch a man in broad daylight.

Link reached down to unclasp the leather cover that enclosed his belt axe as he started through the spruce-walled portion of the trail. Branches brushed both his arms, and swept against his hat. Behind him followed the terrified dogs, with Yuke in the lead and Tibby bringing up the rear. Link rounded a grove of trees where the trail bent, and had just straightened out again when he heard Tibby scream.

It was a shrill, desperate scream that broke off in the middle as though a heavy cloth had suddenly been stuffed into Tibby's mouth. Link whirled with the .22 in his hand. Yuke, Lud, and Kena were huddled right behind him. Off in the spruces was a furtive rustling, as though a sudden breeze had come up to shake the thick trees. There was no other sound. Again Link reached up to wipe cold sweat from his face.

The wolves had Tibby. On a trail where he had followed within a few feet of his master, they had come up and plucked him as easily as a horned owl plucks a sitting partridge from its branch. Link glanced down the short stretch of narrow trail remaining, and began to run toward the opening. He could not possibly stay here in the spruces. The wolves had come within a few feet, and he had never even heard them. With the terrified dogs at his heels he broke into the clearing, and breathed a little easier.

Here he was not hemmed in. Here was room in which he might move, and swing, and fight back at things which would be real instead of flitting shadows in the spruces. Link took stock of his remaining weapons. Extra cartridges for the .22 had been in Tibby's pack, but the tiny pistol was of little use anyway. Still, he had the pistol with five shots, the belt axe, a hunting knife, and the rifle. He could not shoot that, but if there were any close-quarter fighting it would make a very handy club.

Link approached one of the dead spruces, and with his belt axe knocked off a big armload of branches. He went to another tree, and another, until he had a pile of wood taller than his head. He started a little fire, cooked food for himself, and fed the dogs out of Yuke's pack.

He could not banish the fear from his mind, but he tried to call reason to his aid. Wolves never attacked people. (*What about Chirikov?*) Certainly they would never come near a fire. (*Certainly?*) Of course not. As long as he had plenty of wood to burn, he and the dogs were safe if they stayed near the fire. Tomorrow they would go to Two-Bird Cabin, where there were tools and materials, and he could contrive a makeshift firing pin. A little nail would work temporarily, or one of the tacks that he used to fasten furs on stretchers. Link gripped his rifle. As soon as that was in working order he'd tackle all the wolf packs in the north.

The dogs crouched beside him with their ears and noses attuned to the breeze that came out of the spruces. Link waited, knowing from the dogs' actions that the wolves were still there, still watching. At that hour which is neither night nor day, but a part of both, he saw them.

Like shadows with ever-changing forms and no substance, they floated out of the trees as silently as puffs of smoke, and drifted back and forth through the twilight obscurity at the border of the spruces. Link tried to count them; in the changing light it was impossible to tell what was a wolf and what was not. Then, for a few seconds, he saw one wolf very clearly and drew in his breath.

It was a huge black beast with a white scar on its face and shoulder. Turned sidewise, it regarded him steadily and malevolently. It seemed to know that he had no way of harming it. Link wondered wildly how the wolves knew his rifle was useless, then realized the absurdity of such a supposition. The wolves did not know that he couldn't shoot; they were so desperately hungry that they did not care.

Link stared, fascinated, at the black wolf. Then night closed in and he saw it no more.

He stood beside his fire, heaping wood on it until the flames leaped high and cast their red reflection far out into the snow. Link saw something move in the firelight, and drew the .22 from its holster. But it was only a shadow cast by the flames.

He walked restlessly around and around the fire, one hand on his belt axe and the other never very far from the grip of his .22. He kept searching the darkness beyond the fire's glow, until he felt that this must be some wild and hellish dream. There could be no wolves out there. Wolves just didn't come near fire. Wolves didn't come near men, either.

Again, in memory, he heard Tibby's tortured shriek; he thought he would always hear it whenever he walked through thick spruces. Fatigue began to creep over him, and he sat down near the fire. Yuke crept up to lay with his great head near Link's thigh, but kept looking up to stare into the darkness. Link bit his lower lip. This was not real; it could not be real. He sat quietly, his back to the fire and the .22 across his lap. It seemed to him that he had not dozed, but suddenly he was awakened by another wild shriek.

Link sprang up, the pistol in his hand. Within the circle of firelight he saw two gray wolves with Kena between them. In sudden fury he raised the little gun and shot. The .22 spat its ineffective pellets into the night, and one of the gray wolves dropped Kena to yelp and bite its own flank. Another wolf came from the darkness, seized Kena, then all disappeared into silence. For a moment Link stood looking bitterly at the empty pistol, then raised his hand and threw it at the retreating wolves. It was a futile gesture, but he felt better.

Yuke pointed his muzzle at the black sky and howled mournfully. He paused as though expecting an answer. There was none; nothing but silence out in the blackness beyond the fire's glow. Lud merely crouched quietly, awaiting whatever came. Link looked approvingly at him. With little initiative or desire to lead, Lud would have made a fine lead dog had he possessed those traits. He wished only to go his own way, but he would fight courageously when that way was disputed. Lud seemed to know that he might have to fight here, and perhaps to die even as Tibby and Kena had died, but he accepted that knowledge philosophically.

Link threw another armload of wood on the fire. A shower of sparks rose high in the air to spray down in the snow and hiss themselves into nothingness. He strained his eyes into the darkness, trying to see whatever might be there. Nothing moved. There was no sound. Lud crouched low to the ground, bracing himself on tense feet. He sprang forward in the firelight and came to grips with a gray wolf that, somehow, had stalked unseen into the fire's glow. Link rushed forward, striking with the hatchet and thrusting with the knife. He saw the point of the knife descend on the wolf's back, felt it slide into something that yielded beneath it, and the wolf fell, gasping. The bleeding Lud came back to the fire with him, but when they got there Yuke was gone.

Side by side they stood, the man and the wounded dog, staring into the darkness beyond the eerie glow of the fire. Around them shadows moved, and wolves came to drag away and eat the dead wolf Link had stabbed. Gradually, far too gradually, the soft dawn flung fingers of light across the sky, and Link saw the wolves.

They were all out in the clearing, fifteen lean gray brutes with starved bodies, and the great black leader. Link stared long and searchingly at the black wolf, which did not look like an animal as he had always known animals, but a devil with a wolf's body. It sat steadily, unmoving, and stared back at him.

Link threw another armful of wood on the fire and glanced anxiously at the little supply that remained. He had thought the wolves would go back into the forest when morning came. It was inconceivable that such a pack besiege a human being at all, and doubly preposterous that it should dare do so in broad daylight. He had counted on the wolves leaving so he could get to Two-Bird Cabin and repair his rifle.

But the black wolf sat unmoving in the snow, its fore legs braced and its tail straight behind it. Never did it take its eyes from the man's face.

A gust of wind blew down the trail, carrying a

fine powder of snow with it; the snow screen blew between the fire and the wolves. When Link looked again, he thought the black wolf had come nearer. Desperately he threw more sticks on the fire, and glanced around at the dead spruces. The nearest was only twenty feet away, but he knew he would never get there. The black wolf would pull him down before he did. He could do nothing but wait.

The dying fire began to smoke, and Link threw a few more sticks on. He looked at the sky, knowing that the morning was wearing on and that soon the day would be cut in half. Then the night would come again—only neither he nor Lud would see it, for there was not enough wood to last. The black wolf was afraid of the fire, but he would come when it had died out. Link scraped up the last of his sticks and placed them on the burning embers in front of him. He drew his belt axe from its sheath, and stared at the black wolf.

It was very near now, watching him through eyes in which countless demons seemed to dance. A little way behind the black leader were three of his gray followers. They did not look at Link; their eyes were on the wounded Lud, who waited patiently beside his master. Link swallowed hard when he understood the full significance of the wolves' approach. The black leader had marked him for itself, he realized. As soon as the fire died and the black wolf attacked him, the three gray wolves would kill Lud.

Nervously Link slipped the hatchet back into its sheath and drew his knife. He turned it over and over in his hand, trying to decide which weapon would be more effective when he finally met the wolf. In a wave of sheer terror he re-sheathed the knife and drew the axe.

Then he was suddenly calm. The fight was inevitable; he could not avoid it. He thought of old Pete Roberts, a wise old man who knew how harsh the wilderness could be. A lone man could slip and fall, and die lingeringly because there was no help. Or he could meet the black wolf's pack, as Alex Chirikov had done. Well, sooner or later a family would be coming up the auto road into Masland, seeking an opportunity. Old Pete would give them Link's money, and tell them that a man named Stevens would want them to have it.

The fire burned lower and the black wolf edged nearer. His three gray followers moved up with him, and the others circled restlessly in the background. Within minutes now, the black wolf would leap over the fire, straight at his throat.

The dying embers began to flicker out.

13. The Pay Off

Chiri ate from his hot kill, tearing into the moose's belly cavity for the liver, then gorging himself as only a long-starved dog or wolf can gorge. When he could eat no more he lay down to sleep. Twice he awoke growling, and starved coyotes that had come to feed on the moose went back into the spruces and sat quietly until Chiri should leave.

When Chiri had rested he was no longer hungry; his was the faculty of a wolf, that can go without food for many days, then eat enough to last him through many more lean days. The big wild dog nibbled at the now-frozen moose, and for some time stayed idly near it. Here was food for many days, and instinct bade him stay close by.

At the same time there was something else that pulled him away. It was an uneasiness and anxiety that he did not understand. But when he finally left the moose he went straight back to the cabin on the Gander. It was deserted. For a while, still uneasy and uncertain as to exactly what he should do next, he remained near the empty cabin. But there was a different factor connected with his being here than there had ever been before; the chain was no longer about his neck. He was free to do as he chose.

Slowly he followed Link's trail away from the cabin. Then he came to the place where the black wolf and his pack had taken up their stalk of Link and his dogs, and the new scent gave wings to his legs. Everything except the black wolf was forgotten.

Chiri flashed on, into the narrow trail through the spruces, past the spot where Tibby had been slain, out into the meadow. He scarcely noticed either Link or the wounded Lud as he leaped over the almost-dead fire. He stood there, his feet braced solidly and his body straining forward. His eagerness to join the battle was tempered with good sense.

His pointed muzzle was up, his yellow eyes half-closed, as every nerve and muscle in his body quivered with his effort to control himself. No snarl curved his lips, no growl rumbled from his chest, as he studied the black wolf which still sat twenty yards from the fire, flanked by its three gray followers.

Now the black wolf's eyes went from Link Stevens to Chiri. His tongue ran out, and his mouth seemed to form a mocking laugh that bespoke his hate of man and his contempt for the dogs that belonged to man. The black wolf read this dog's intention of fighting him as clearly as he read the stories left in deer tracks. He would still kill the man, but first he would kill the dog. And he would do it alone. Some invisible message passed from him to the three gray wolves. They swung about and trotted farther away to join the rest of the pack.

The black wolf's followers sat in a grim semicircle, fierce and cold-blooded spectators of the battle they knew was coming. The wolves shuffled their front paws expectantly, and began to drool. There would be blood on the snow, and warm meat to fill their lean bellies.

Chiri uttered a single deep-throated growl. It strained from his chest, and seemed to ripple out between his fangs in a solid, bubbling stream. It told the black wolf of Chiri's hate, a hate greater even than the black wolf's own. It told of the battle of the windfall, where his mother and his two brothers had died. It told of the flight through the gorge, and the puppy's fear and frustration because he had had to run away. And it warned the black wolf that vengeance was about to descend upon him.

The black wolf's grin widened, as if he had heard such threats before, as if he were reminding this presumptuous dog that previous challengers were dead, while the black wolf was still alive.

Then they joined the battle.

It was no sudden rush, no quick collision of two leaping bodies as they sought to knock each other off their feet. Chiri went forward as a cat stalks a mouse, carrying the fight to the black wolf. Deliberately Chiri held his head high, knowing that the wolf would seek to take advantage of this weakness. Slowly he closed the distance between them, feeling out his fierce enemy as he advanced.

When the black wolf came in, he moved like rippling black water. The devils in his eyes danced frantically, for the dog was holding his head too high and his throat was exposed. Feinting, as though he were going to slide past and attack from the flank, the black wolf dived suddenly for that unprotected throat.

But it was not there. Chiri swerved to one side

and brought his head suddenly down. As he did so, his long fangs sliced through the black wolf's cheek. Red blood bubbled down to stain the black fur. The wolf wheeled away, champing his teeth to eject the hair clinging to them. But hair was all they had found; his thrust at Chiri's throat had failed completely.

They stood five feet apart, facing each other, while each revised his plan of action from what he had learned from the initial skirmish. The black wolf examined every inch of Chiri's body, trying for another weak spot. In the very absence of scars or injuries, the wolf saw the greatest weakness of all.

The dog was young, and therefore inexperienced. Like a master boxer the black wolf began to play on that inexperience, dashing in and out again, luring the dog into making short, ineffective rushes. As soon as Chiri became sufficiently confused, then would come the black wolf's time. Then he could kill again as he had killed before.

For a moment Chiri stood still, studying this new maneuver and trying to discover the reasons for it. He made a little half-jump forward, but did not fling himself wholeheartedly at the wolf. Born wild, he had all the caution of any wild thing. Behind that was the inborn wisdom of his mother and his staghound father, who in turn had inherited that wisdom from dogs who had been bred for intelligence as well as strength and speed. Consequently, when the black wolf finally did come in, Chiri was not unprepared.

He whirled, taking the rush meant for his soft flank on his ribbed chest. The black wolf's teeth, razor-edged knives in a vise-strong jaw, slashed and left a gaping wound in the dog's shoulder.

Chiri yielded to the attack, going backward as the wolf came forward; but even as he gave ground he acted.

He ducked his jaws to the black wolf's front leg, and would have bitten it in two had the thrust gone home. But the black wolf was a master of this game of killing and keeping from being killed. He drew back, and Chiri's teeth severed only the muscles in the front part of the leg.

Farther out in the clearing the gray wolves were on their feet, straining forward but taking no part. By the fire Link stood spellbound, breathlessly watching this battle that must end in the death of one or both fighters. Even the wounded Lud was sitting up to watch, his eyes fixed on the dog whom he had long known as his real leader.

Suddenly the black wolf rushed again, flinging himself across the space that separated him from Chiri, intending to bear him down by sheer force. The dog braced himself to meet the rush. For a moment they were very close, parrying fang with fang and rearing to fight with claws and teeth.

When the black wolf broke away, he knew that Chiri was his equal. He knew too that he had to kill. If he did not, his own pack would be upon him like one wolf with fifteen sets of fangs. They would tear him apart because he was defeated, and no longer fit to lead. The wolf turned back with a snarl toward the hated mask-face that had escaped him as a puppy and now challenged his best efforts.

Again Chiri stalked cat-footed across the space that separated them. The black wolf met him fang to fang, and again they stood slashing and parrying. The wolf struck at Chiri's head, missed, and sliced off the top of one of the big dog's pointed ears. Blood ebbed down the side of Chiri's head. He shook it to get the blood out of his eye.

Seizing the opportunity, the black wolf rushed suddenly, striking Chiri's wounded shoulder with his own, and the dog went down. The gray wolves rose expectantly, ready to rush in and finish what their leader had started. Slowly, disappointedly, they settled down again; resilient as rubber, Chiri was up and facing the black wolf. And this time both realized the mighty weapon that was on the dog's side, a weapon more powerful than any the black wolf had now or ever could have again—youth.

When he had first attained his own maturity, the black wolf had been agile as a willow switch, tough as a hickory limb, tireless as running water. But there had been a great many trails since then, much brutal slaying, many terrible fights, many long, lean winters. The black wolf had accumulated vast experience, but nothing could change the fact that he was old. And being old, he could not withstand the repeated attacks of a younger animal whose strength was equal to his own.

Chiri had felt his enemy give ground. It was nothing that could be seen, just a scrap of trampled snow that the wolf yielded. But he had yielded because he could not do otherwise. Chiri pressed his advantage furiously, and the black wolf gave more ground.

Coming in again, the wolf carried the fight with the fury of desperation. He had battled many things, and seen them lying dead on the snow. Always he had been contemptuous of animals weaker than he. Now that he had met something stronger, the black wolf knew that he must either win or lie dead on the snow himself. Because he was desperate, for the first time he was also reckless.

Chiri met him head on, parrying his fangs, ducking, feinting. The black wolf dived at his front leg. Slashing, he leaped back and almost at once came in again. Chiri balanced his wounded leg on the snow, and lunged forward. It was a swift and unexpected maneuver, and it took the black wolf by surprise. Leaping forward himself, he went almost straight into Chiri's jaws.

The dog slashed once, and felt his fangs go cleanly through skin and muscle, into the black wolf's throat. The devils in the wolf's eyes no longer danced; for the first time there was fear in his eyes, fear of the death that he had brought to so many others. He turned and tried to run, but there was a suddenly opened faucet in his throat, through which blood rushed to spill on the trampled snow. The black wolf staggered and went down. He tried to rise again and could not.

The ring of gray wolves rose eagerly, anxiously, ready to come in and tear their own defeated leader to bits. But Chiri limped to the body of the black wolf and reared with his paws upon it. He looked toward the gray pack and it subsided. A new leader had come. By right of strength his was the position that the black despot had held for so many years. By the law of the pack he ruled, and the pack must await his pleasure.

For the first time Chiri swung his head to look back at Link Stevens.

Link stood breathlessly, one hand on the wounded Lud's head. He too knew what was taking place; the decision would be Chiri's alone. Slowly, deliberately, the dog turned from the black wolf and walked toward the man. He was a dog, and dogs chose men. The gray wolves melted silently into the forest.

For a moment Link remained where he was, too stunned to move. He had won after all, won when he thought he had lost. Gone was the deadly fear that had driven him out of the Gander. He felt supremely confident, sure of himself, sure of his future. His lost faith had returned.

Link laid his hand on the dog's head. "Come on, Chiri," he said.

Together they went down the trail, Link and Lud side by side, Chiri in the lead.

ABOUT THE AUTHOR

JIM KJELGAARD's first book was *Forest Patrol* (1941), based on the wilderness experiences of himself and his brother, a forest ranger. Since then he has written many others—all of them concerned with the out-of-doors. *Big Red, Irish Red,* and *Outlaw Red* are dog stories about Irish setters. *Kalak of the Ice* (a polar bear) and *Chip, the Dam Builder* (a beaver) are wild-animal stories. *Snow Dog* and *Wild Trek* describe the adventures of a trapper and his half-wild dog. *Haunt Fox* is the story both of a fox and of the dog and boy who trailed him, and *Stormy* is concerned with a wildfowl retriever and his young owner. *Fire-Hunter* is a story about prehistoric man; *Boomerang Hunter* about the equally primitive Australian aborigine. *Rebel Siege* and *Buckskin Brigade* are tales of American frontiersmen, and *Wolf Brother* presents the Indian side of "the winning of the West." The cougar-hunting *Lion Hound* and the greyhound story, *Desert Dog,* are laid in the present-day Southwest. *A Nose for Trouble* and *Trailing Trouble* are adventure mysteries centered around a game warden and his man-hunting bloodhound. The same game warden also appears in *Wildlife Cameraman* and *Hidden Trail,* stories about a young nature photographer and his dog.

JIM KJELGAARD

In these adventure stories, Jim Kjelgaard shows us the special world of animals, the wilderness, and the bonds between men and dogs. *Irish Red* and *Outlaw Red* are stories about two champion Irish setters. *Snow Dog* shows what happens when a half-wild dog crosses paths with a trapper. The cougar-hunting *Lion Hound* and the greyhound story *Desert Dog* take place in our present-day Southwest. And, *Stormy* is an extraordinary story of a boy and his devoted dog. You'll want to read all these exciting books.

☐ 15456	A NOSE FOR TROUBLE	$2.50
☐ 15368	HAUNT FOX	$2.25
☐ 15434	BIG RED	$2.95
☐ 15324	DESERT DOG	$2.50
☐ 15286	IRISH RED: SON OF BIG RED	$2.50
☐ 15427	LION HOUND	$2.95
☐ 15339	OUTLAW RED	$2.50
☐ 15365	SNOW DOG	$2.50
☐ 15388	STORMY	$2.50
☐ 15466	WILD TREK	$2.75

<u>Prices and availability subject to change without notice.</u>

FROM THE SPOOKY, EERIE PEN OF JOHN BELLAIRS . . .

☐ **THE CURSE OF THE**   15540/$2.95
  BLUE FIGURINE

Johnny Dixon knows a lot about ancient Egypt and curses and evil spirits—but when he finds the blue figurine, he actually "sees" a frightening, super-natural world. Even his friend Professor Childermass can't help him!

☐ **THE MUMMY, THE WILL**   15498/$2.75
  AND THE CRYPT

For months Johnny has been working on a riddle that would lead to a $10,000 reward. Feeling certain that the money is hidden somewhere in the house of a dead man, Johnny goes into his house where a bolt of lightning reveals to him that the house is not quite deserted . . .

☐ **THE SPELL OF THE**   15357/$2.50
  SORCERER'S SKULL

Johnny Dixon is back, but this time he's not teamed up with Dr. Childermass. That's because his friend, the Professor, has disappeared!

Shop at home
for quality children's books
and save money, too.

Now you can order books for the whole family from Bantam's latest catalog of hundreds of titles including many fine children's books. *And* this special offer gives you an opportunity to purchase a Bantam book for only 50¢. Here's how:

By ordering any five books at the regular price per order, you can also choose any other single book listed (up to a $5.95 value) for just 50¢. Some restrictions do apply, so for further details send for Bantam's catalog of titles today.